Bought With Blood

By Brian Potter

STHENOTYPE

Cover art by Billie Hopple
Editing by Stepheni Potter and Michael Allen

First Edition 2023

ISBN 979-8-9873772-5-3

Published by SthenoType
Medford, NJ 08055
www.SthenoType.com

Nothing will do it justice, I've had a massive amount of help and support. I love you all.

You said, "I can't tell you what you should do. That's never worked before. So stop talking about it, and go do it."

Thanks, Dad. I'm doing it.

En Garde (Prologue; 2003)

The breeze carried a simple conversation with his steady breath on the chilly November night. Each exhale was a hot mist that pushed against, then mingled with, the darkness; they disagreed and then calmly settled. A few stars distantly cast light where the clouded moon could not as Simon looked on in silent frustration with his thoughts.

He had come to the familiar quaint graveyard as he had many times before. It was a place he could collect himself and his thoughts before he'd go to watch over the home where he had grown up so many years ago.

He fought with himself over the memory of having left this place. Simon replaced the dried flowers under her name as he always had before and returned the wide-brimmed, worn fedora to his brow with a nod before he took his leave. He shook his head abruptly like he was fighting off fatigue or his memories or both. Then with no urgency, he turned to go and walked down the street of his old neighborhood.

Simon rounded the corner from the church house where the recent addition and new sign were placed. He could already see the driveway where he learned to ride a bicycle. The space at the curb where his father's family sedan used to park had been repaved over the summer. The fresh tarmac burned his nostrils when he had come here then. There were no more cracks and holes near the edges of the roads; it all had a new makeover, despite so many of the same, aged as they were, features like the siding of the corner house he passed that still carried a very dated, subtle green. It was clean but drab as ever and held the trend of a generation before with its somewhat tacky horizontal aluminum siding slats.

When Simon crossed the street, a small singular headlight caught his attention. It belonged to a tiny silver motorbike parked at the edge of the drive upon which his sights were set. It was a late hour, which brought his dissonant fraternal instinct into motion since no doubt it was his now grown sister who hopped off the bike and started up the walk. Simon slowed his pace and lingered nearer to shadows so he could watch without notice. In aggravation, the young woman threw her hands out from the waist. He could see the locked door had stopped her. She looked to one side and then the other and reached up to pull her hair back, then moved to a low window and raised the pane before she pulled herself inside head first.

If he were confident it could be anyone else, he might have rushed to stop her to secure his father's home. He momentarily looked on from the dark before she reemerged from the front door. She carefully kept it from slamming closed before the latch clicked into place. She jogged back to her little bike, pulled the strap under her chin, and threw her leg over to kick the park stand away. For a moment, she looked up at the house, and with a drop of her chin, she returned the tilted bar into place to leave the vehicle standing. She dismounted into a run and returned to the open window, then pulled down against the seal. It seemed to stick at first, then came down fast and caused something inside to drop and break.

"Dammit!" she cried as she sprinted back, vaulted onto the seat, and sped away with the little engine whirring to gain speed.

A few seconds later, a man's broad frame filled the open door's space, pushed at the screen door, and hurriedly stepped out onto the lawn in little clothing. His thinning hair stood at one side, and he hung his head in disappointment and helplessness. Simon must have been staring too hard as the older man's attention seemed to draw straight to his hidden location. He held fast and waited as his father finally turned and trudged back inside the house defeated, quietly closing the door.

Simon deeply inhaled the mix of aromas, barely catching each from afar. Leila's perfume, coupled with his father's pipe tobacco breath amidst the exhaust trail.

As soon as the inside lights went out, Simon stepped back out of the bushes and into the street. At a run, he followed the cemented path to the cemetery and slid onto the torn leather seat of an old jeep. He slammed the clutch and cranked the key a forward turn until the motor spun its revolutions high, then flat-shifted to catch up with Leila. He no longer had the luxury of her fragrance to follow but the advantage of late night in a quiet neighborhood which allowed him to soon see the single tiny red tail light ahead. After only six blocks, he wound the wheel left to chase her scooter out of the borough. He kept his distance as they approached the main road toward the bridge that led to the city limits.

Through the specked windshield, he could see the skyline as it came into view over the river. The lights were nearly blinding against the glare on the jeep's flat windshield. Once she was across the bridge, Leila turned again toward the business district. Several street signs blurred as they drove toward the northern edge of town. She slowed one block from the T-stop end of the street and leaned into a parking lot at the Rougir de Vie. It was a gentleman's club in a part of town where the remaining businesses were mostly privately owned, and many were run-down.

Simon parked down the street, outside a nearby hotel, and watched until she emerged from the building nearly an hour later. When she came outside, she was escorted by a tall, thin man on foot hastily headed south. She looked like she had trouble walking at first, but as he held her close, the purchase in her steps returned. They entered a small sedan and began to leave the lot. A second, more muscular man with a curling mullet stepped out from the building after them. He looked down the sidewalk in their direction, then ran back into the club out of sight.

Simon waited only a minute and then started the engine again. As he turned around to see where the couple was headed, he was cut off by a biker peeling out of the club's parking area. The bike's engine loudly echoed through the tall buildings with an eery, cacophonous growl in the quiet, late hour. Simon turned and corrected the steering wheel to tail them. He soon found the motorcycle parked outside a subway station just a few blocks away. Simon parked nearby and hurried down the concrete steps that led under the city.

As Simon reached the bottom-most landing, he saw and recognized the biker. "Blake?" he asked himself, barely above a whisper.

Under the fluorescent bar bulbs in the station, he could see Blake was trying to talk to Leila, to convince her of something that was not sinking in at all. She leered back at him from an arm's length with wide eyes and tilted her head slightly to one side like a patient predator bird.

Her body was poised and aggressive with her shoulders forward, yet she seemed to draw no breath in her heated state. She circled and sized him up as he spoke, determining the challenge before she made each calculated step. Blake seemed to be losing the argument to silence, and when he lost patience threw his hands out at his sides much the way she had hours earlier with a short, thick steam blast from his nostrils.

He puffed out his chest and leaned toward her long enough to shout, "Fine! Go then, you ungrateful bitch!" Then he turned from her, conceding.

Simon saw her animalistic sneer raise in advantage as the vulnerable opportunity became present. He immediately leaped past the ticket booth to try to intervene as Leila lunged at her target and latched onto his broad back. Her tiny fingers pulled Blake's face to one side and dug her nails across his cheek.

She bit down deep into his neck as he struggled and writhed. He yelled out with surprise and pain and looked up at Simon's face in shock and confusion. Her narrowed and lifeless doll eyes looked up, solidly blackened at the intruder as Simon advanced. Blood spilled, soaking her lips along with Blake's shoulder and white T-shirt as she savagely pierced his flesh.

Leila dropped down and pushed her victim into Simon as she turned to flee, seeing the numbers turn against her favor. Simon looked around as he and Blake collided to see no one else anywhere in the cool, cavernous station. Not his little sister nor the tall man who led her here. The rail cars approached with a steely scream and obscured the tunnel from view, leaving him no choice but to tend to the wounds at his old friend's collar.

Blake stood bleeding in anger, looked around quickly, and his sights landed on his shoulder as his shirt and leather jacket soaked with the red stain.

"What the hell was that?" he shouted into the station to be sure she could hear. "After everything I've done for you, this is my thanks?"

Simon turned back to him and pulled a handkerchief to press into the torn flesh. "Don't move," he ordered. "You're still bleeding."

"Yeah? And just who the fuck are you? My god-damned hero? Come to save the day before little Miss Princess digs her nails into me some more?"

"It wasn't just her nails. She bit you," Simon corrected him and surprised himself with the reality of the attack.

"Oh yeah? Bit me, huh? So what? You're some kind of referee for little bitch fights?" Blake pushed Simon away and went on shouting, "Get off me! I ain't hurt!"

Blake deflected every attempt Simon made to speak or help as his anger flared and barked at Simon. He winced in pain briefly as he pulled off the saturated, square cloth and tossed it away as more blood flowed from the wound. He took a deep breath, then another, and collapsed heavily at Simon's feet.

After one last look into the subway, Simon set to work to drag the biker out of the station back to his vehicle. With a spare shirt from his duffel, Simon did his best to dress the wound and lay Blake back in the passenger seat so he could drive them back to the club.

Once there, Simon parked outside in the unlit parking lot near the door so he could help Blake inside more easily. Blake's brow furrowed under pain and confusion, with a fresh bandage on his naked shoulder and a wet towel stained with his blood over the other, as he poured straight bourbon into two small glasses.

Blake gestured with his empty glass after having taken the slug, and he pried again, "You still didn't tell me why you were following her in the first place."

Simon stared emptily into the caramel drink before him. He exhaled slowly and offered, "I told you, I haven't seen her in a long time. About a year, I guess. And the way she just left her father standing there, I figured she must be running away."

Simon picked up the shot and brought it under his nose but didn't drink. Instead, he dipped his finger, rubbed it into his bottom lip, and familiarized the taste and smell. The flavor was semi-sweet within the warmth, even on the tip of his tongue, and the aroma was neither foul nor pleasant but strong and distinct.

"She's only a kid," Simon sighed.

"No need to put a nipple on that," Blake taunted. "It's my preferred swig, so I keep plenty on hand." He reached under the bar, retrieved a polo shirt with the club logo, and pulled it over his head. He then poured another even ounce into his glass and returned the bottle to its place, with the label routinely faced forward. "So, what about the bite, then," he prodded. "You ever see anything like that?"

Simon's eyes peered into Blake's for a lingering moment to help him find the answer on his own. His lips moved a few times and drew breath to utter the difficult, if not impossible, truth.

Simon finally broke the confused silence. "Look, I know you're not gonna believe me, but that guy she was with is… a vampire." His words escaped his lips like ripping off a band-aid.

Blake's expression glazed a moment as he heard the word. An unsettling shiver reached over him and chilled a space between his shoulders up into his hairline. He stepped forward and leaned over the hardwood bar before he stretched his arms out to brace his upper body weight, then searched into Simon's somber, gray stare. He finally released a long, uneasy sigh and shook his head.

"I have every reason to walk away from this right now. I could call it bullshit and leave you to your shadows and nightmares," Blake half-joked. "You know that, right? How crazy this sounds?" His effort to bluff was not fruitful, as Simon sat unwaveringly. He stood straight again, shook his head, and finally looked away.

"But you should know," Simon began, "I have no reason to exaggerate something like this." He stood also and carefully replaced the stool upside down on the countertop. "So I'm going to start looking for this guy. With or without you. It doesn't have to be your problem if you think it's better to just wait here and do nothing until she-"

Blake cut in, his temper slightly unsettled. "I didn't say I was out. I didn't even say I didn't believe what you said." He finally made eye contact again and asked, "But how do we go after someone or something like that?"

Blake grabbed a bar mop, soaking it in hot water from the sink behind the bar, wrung it out, and blotted it into the bloodstain on his leather jacket as it draped over one arm.

A moment of awkward silence passed before Simon pulled a heavy handgun from his concealed shoulder harness and rolled the revolving chamber a few slots before he returned it snugly under his coat into the worn holster.

With a slight shrug, Simon offered, "I figure if we start now, we're already following a cold trail at best. But she's your sister too, so if you have any ideas of where to begin, I'm open to suggestions."

"Don't call her that," Blake replied coldly. "If I was anything to her, she wouldn't have left."

November, 2011

"You could be dead up on that stage and those animals would still be howling," came a remark from one of Rougir de Vie's more seasoned dancers. Another replied, "It sure is rowdy out there."

Tanya was trying to stay out of the way of the curtain as the two chatting women came through in just their high heels and g-strings. They carried their stage outfits and brushed past her to sit in front of their assigned vanity stations to touch up before their next set. A second pair of girls rushed through the curtain as another song cued up, nearly knocking her over.

One of them chided Tanya over her shoulder, "Watch it, new blood."

"Tanya, help me. We're up next!" Melissa stood with her back turned, trying to hold onto the ties of her pink fluorescent bikini top behind her back.

Tanya stepped across the entry to her dance partner, Melissa, and pulled the ties together across her back. She made a simple slipknot and spun Melissa around to help her into a slinky white net dress that barely reached her thighs. Tanya stole a look into a nearby mirror to flip her feathery blonde hair around a bit. Then she pulled her own silvery sheer tank dress on over a reflective blue halter and strappy matched bottom. She spun to check the line on her stockings up the back when she heard a man's voice that boomed through the public address system.

"Gentlemen, take a seat up front for our very own tantalizing twins, Angel and Rose!" The PA speaker squelched with a bit of feedback.

Tanya took a deep breath and gave a nod to Melissa as they pushed through the curtain. Just as they took their steps onto the stage together, Tanya commented how much she liked having a stage name as she often did. "Playing a character makes me want to do plays again like we used to."

The dancers walked out in tandem, almost serpent-like, getting their first look at the crowd for their shift. Blinding lights cut across the stage in swirls, and the girls held each other with arms behind the others' back until they reached the edge of the thrust. The music was loud, but the men were even louder. Cheers and whistles came at them from every direction as Tanya and Melissa faced each other waving their arms at their sides like sea creatures. As the beat dropped, they turned with their backs to each other, and each bent at the waist with stretched palms out on the stage floor. When they stood again, they stepped in beat with the music away from each other to address the room with heavy hip-swaying movements.

As rehearsed, the women turned to face each other again from opposite ends. They waved their fingers at one another before pulling up the hem of their dresses to remove their outer layers, which had done little to cover them. With a hair flip, they approached the center pole together, where Tanya spun to fling her leg up around the pole as Melissa stretched low in front for a cat-like pose. Tanya reached down to untie Melissa's bikini top, as Melissa reached up to untie Tanya's halter. They used their next few steps in the dance to fluidly peel away their tops and switched stage sides to get closer to the men waiting with dollar bills held high.

Their first song was ending, and a faster one started. This was their cue to make their rounds to the rest of the men in front waiting to get a closer look. Unlike the first song, during this one, Tanya and Melissa took more time at each position, posing their bodies low and within reach to tempt each potential viewer.

Tanya felt her gaze pulled toward the far corner of the room, over and over. Each time she looked into the space, a man seated there fixed his eyes on her and continued to stare back. He was dressed far too well for this place in a silvery sport coat and red tie. She caught a second glance at him during a turn and saw him pass a pack of folded bills to a nearby bouncer as he pointed toward the stage. The song was welling up to its last verse. Tanya shook her head free of the distraction, taking long, leggy strides past her last few customers near the stage and plucking their dollar bills away with a wink or blown kiss in place of the show of skin they came to see.

Before she had a chance to retrieve her dress and top from the stage, Melissa had beaten her to it and smacked her across her exposed backside, eliciting cheers and whistles from the crowd as the dancers walked back through the curtain just as the music hit its last beat.

"Okay, tell me you saw that guy," Tanya said, pushing through the curtain, almost slamming into one of the other dancers trying to get past them for their set. "Sorry, my fault."

Melissa tossed the dresses at Tanya with a laugh. "You must be joking. There's a full house out there, and you want me to notice one guy?" She grinned at herself in the mirror smugly. "How many would be disappointed if I only paid attention to one?"

"Right, I get it," Tanya submitted. "I just, I don't know. I felt him watching, like boring into my soul. Drawing my eyes to him." She kicked off her backless heels and sat down next to Melissa. "It's weird, but he's the first guy that made me feel... naked up there."

A few of the other girls listening in laughed out loud but were cut off by a gravelly male voice. "Chat after hours, ladies. Angel, Rose, pick something nice to wear for a VIP show." Blake flashed a fan of money and tossed it in front of Melissa, where her makeup kit lay open. "They paid for a half hour, and I charged double because I can't spare anyone for longer than fifteen minutes with a mob like that out there. But if they want more, charge the same again. It's all yours if they spring for it."

"Mr. Gentry," said a young dancer as she adjusted her shining, blue, bobbed wig to frame her round mocha-colored face. "You said no men in the dressing room."

Blake leaned over her, close to her face, and grinned. "Security goes anywhere we feel the need. Can never be too

safe. Besides, there's nothing here I haven't seen on stage."
He whispered something in her ear and then turned to leave.
"You got three sets to get to the Champagne Room, ladies,"
he reminded, looking up at Tanya. "Put on your best. We
need more of that kind of money in here."

Tanya turned to the hanger racks, picked a set of costumes
for Melissa and herself, and passed a pleather black cincher to
Melissa.

"Why do I always have to be the bad twin?" Melissa pouted
as she pulled on a red negligee.

Tanya faked a laugh. "Because I make the outfits, and mine
don't fit you, and yours don't fit me. Besides, you are the bad
child. Mom and Dad told me so." She stuck out her tongue
and winked at Melissa's reflection in the mirror.

Melissa added a line of black to her eyelids and clapped back.
"Pssh! I bet Mommy and Daddy would change their tune real
quick if they found out this job was your idea."

"Now, don't give me that. I never forced you to do this. You
asked me how I was making so much money, and you wanted
in on it," Tanya told her. "Besides, you know this is only
temporary until we get through school. Which reminds me,
you haven't reapplied yet and-"

The blue-haired dancer pushed her chair back loudly, huffed
with a look at the stack of bills on the vanity, and hurried out
of the dressing room.

"Hey, Missy," Tanya started again in a hushed tone while buttoning herself into a white velour corset top. "Tuck that money away. I don't like the way she was looking over here. A half-hour is plenty of time to lose our rent money."

Melissa rolled off her net stockings and stepped into a pair of red heels, then stuffed their folded money into one of the white thigh-high boots Tanya would be wearing. "Can't get much safer than that in this place, am I right, Angel?" She stepped behind Tanya and draped a feathered white boa over her shoulders.

Tanya fixed a wide, white headband into place and fanned her hair out over it to resemble a halo, then pushed a horned headband into Melissa's hair, looking into her face with worry. "Hey, be careful, okay? That guy gave me the creeps. And I think he's our private show customer." She hugged her sister just long enough for the thumping song to end.

A Match Made in High Heels

Just walking through the door made Simon flinch slightly as a wave of perfumes, liquors, sweat, and dirty money swirled about in the small space. The dull, tan paneling in the corridor held tacked and taped fliers promoting drink specials, local concerts, and ads from local businesses, many of which were outdated. Heavy beats from the sound system thumped against his inner ear and reverberated against the thin interior walls. This entryway had one dim tube light that was fighting to stay lit, and beyond it, the main room was a deep, bruised purple of black lighting.

The secondary door was propped open, and as Simon stepped through it, he was met by a squat, sausage-fingered man whose glowing, yellow SECURITY shirt couldn't tuck in the front. Simon asked where he could find the owner. Under a sweat-glossed and bald head, the doorman's blond eyebrows floated to receive the question and then furled as he thumb-pointed over his shoulder behind the bar.

A dazzling spread of laser lights from a twisting ceiling fixture offended Simon's eyes as he narrowed them and quickly strode across the room. Flirting waitresses in belly-tied tees and swaggering men of all shapes and persuasions cluttered the room at nearly full capacity. Saturday nights always were busy around eleven o'clock.

A tiny brunette girl was posing and undulating on the bar top to sell body shots. Spots of what smelled like tequila, amaretto, and other liquors stained her stretched neon green bikini, and droplets formed in her cleavage and appeared like morning dew on the fine hairs of her taut belly. Her lime-painted eyes looked around to see if anyone else was closer, then landed again on Simon as she folded her hands behind her head under the tight bun in her hair.

"Come on, sugar, it's just five bucks a shot, anywhere you like. Can't beat that," she offered.

He removed his hat and stared at her momentarily, deciding carefully on his words, then reached into his pocket, separating a five from a couple of ones. He raked his hair away from his face, then dropped the bill and said, "I don't drink, but serve one up to the guy in charge, would ya?"

She sat up on her knees, letting her hands slowly fall to take the money and folding it in half lengthwise. She pushed it into the side of her purple garter with an organized cluster of cash.

She looked back up at Simon, then over her shoulder to a windowed office door, and shouted, "Hey, Mr. Gentry! Somebody wants to buy you a shot!"

A few seconds later, the door swung in, and Blake came out, his big smile fading to a smirk when he saw who was waiting. Another girl with a blue, bobbed wig quickly left the office. She turned away, smoothing a black, shark bite mini-dress into place over a tiny G-string that matched her hair, and let the door close behind her.

The bar top brunette tried to regain their attention, "Come on now, the gentleman already paid." She was still almost shouting to be heard over the music in the room.

"The usual then," Blake said aloud as he grabbed a bottle of shining brown liquor.

She spread her knees out and arched her back, pushing her tan-lined little breasts up, and licked her glossy, candy-apple lips while trying to seduce Simon with her eyes again as a reminder that she acknowledged him as the paying customer.

Blake brushed his hand up the back of her neck, roughly took a fistful of her hair, pulled down to tilt her head back, and poured a smooth double into her mouth. He let a few seconds pass until he saw her struggling to not swallow and then bent over her and slid his tongue into her mouth until their lips sealed. They held a moment, and she inhaled sharply through her nostrils, with her ribs pressing out past her flat tummy. A bit of liquid escaped and trickled down her cheek before he finally let go. Her eyes smoldered up at him and then at Simon as she let out a breath between pursed lips, licking slowly across them again. Her pencil eraser nipples grew hard, and her skin goose-bumped all over.

Blake tossed a tiny garment onto the bar for the girl and pointed to the stage. "Your set is next," he said. Then he stepped over to the door while looking back at Simon and directed, "My office." As he pushed the door open, waiting, he looked across to his security at the entrance, patting down a group of men in suits. He looked back into the corner to give a nod to the men who had just paid for a private show.

"Oh yeah. We're gonna do fine tonight. Look at all that money that just came in."

Simon sniffed the air again, catching something out of place that made his nose wrinkle. The smell was weak between the other scents in the room, though coupled with the perfumes and sweat, he had to shake away its dizzying effect. He held fast a moment, perusing the room for the offender. In front of him were a pair of dancers, a blonde and an unnatural redhead known on stage as Angel and Rose, dressed in angel and devil costume lingerie, respectively. They moved past him to quickly greet some men who looked out of place in their tailored suits. The girls were escorting the well-dressed men immediately to the VIP area as if they had an appointment.

When Simon followed Blake through the door, he was met with a fresh wave of smells. The dull, piss-colored walls of the office held only a square clock, multiple screens viewing the club's security feeds, and years of nicotine residue with an acrid aroma to match. The muffled, thumping beat persisted from outside the door as Blake went to a leather-backed chair that rolled behind a desk comprising two filing cabinets with a poker table top. Several takeout containers were open on the tabletop, with disposable utensils stuck out from some of them. He unlocked a drawer and pulled what looked like a thick, rubber band-wrapped file, and slid it across the green felt.

"How is it you've been coming here eight years and still don't drink?" Blake was asking but paying more attention to the cigarette he was lighting than the other man in the room. He flopped the lighter onto the table and let loose a long blast of nostril smoke. He twisted his neck uncomfortably and pulled his broad empty hand across the scar concealed beneath his beard like easing a stiff muscle. Simon pulled photos and clippings from the file as he had done so many times. He only looked up from the table with an annoyed glare when Blake paused long enough to make room for a reply. "I gotta admit, though, it doesn't taste like it used to. It's funny how the first one I ever had was so terrible. And I remember the way it burned down my throat and made me wonder how anyone could want to drink all the time."

Blake stubbed out his smoke and pushed aside the ashtray as the butt smoldered. "Look, I don't want to throw in the towel any more than you do-"

"Then don't," Simon cut him short and tossed the articles back together in a pile.

Simon pushed back from the table and pulled a thick rubber band around the folder, and left it near a cracked chip pocket on the table. He turned and pulled the door open, looking across to the still-occupied VIP room, and noticed there was no security placed there.

Simon asked, "You do private parties with no eyes on the room now, too?"

A scream broke out from where he was looking, and Simon instinctively rushed to the unguarded door. Finding it locked, Simon slammed his shoulder into the wood with full force, splintering the cheap wood through the frame. In the first second that he had to take in the scene, both the girls were being held down, but the Kool-Aid redhead girl was lying still and possibly unconscious. The blonde girl could barely struggle and whine at her attacker by the time Simon reached out to grab him. That awful mixed smell of copper and chalk, more powerful now, caught him again as he looked into the face of a monster. His nostrils flared with steady stinging hate, and his eyes went wide and rolled back into his head.

The man that Simon grabbed bared blood-stained fangs like a wild animal, ready to defend its fresh kill. His face drew a pale porcelain color as his fingernails pointed into thin, miniature stilettos. The suited man hissed his warning at Simon, "Wrong party, friend."

Simon's long coat slipped off his shoulders, and his clothes were already melding into muscle and coarse hair. His spine popped, broke, and transformed, letting a brown-grey pelt take over his entire body. His ears grew and pushed back across his skull, taking on a pointed shape. Curling, dark razors tipped his paw hands and spread wide to either side of him as the changes continued. His knuckles, arms, and legs became twists of sinew and cartilage just before they slipped into a low crackling of joint remembrance and covered over themselves with thick hair. Terrible, long, spit-dripping canines bore out from a grizzled maw and snapped and gaped in a fierce growling bed of wet, black gums. He raised on his haunches, looked down the head in height he'd grown, and stared with empty black eyes at his opponent.

The blonde stripper was thrown into the corner against a sharp pillar fixture as her attacker turned to square off with Simon. The other girl was splayed out, face up and mouth agape on one of the low-reclining chairs that resembled a plush high-heeled shoe as the vampire over her also rounded to face the intruder. The naked redhead didn't move as both vampires in suits moved to attack the morphing beast who had interrupted them.

Blake had only been a few steps behind Simon but stopped to grab the undercounter shotgun, then slid to a stop in the doorway to fire one shot into the side of the nearest suit, who was already airborne, lunging at Simon from the right. The searing pellets were buried in the ribs of his target and threw the attacker sprawling to the floor. Glasses broke as everyone in the club suddenly dropped, with many screaming and looking toward the cacophonous gun blast. He pumped the barrel action, discharging the empty shell, then quickly ducked away from the opening in the doorway when the hissing man leaped back to his feet. Blake tried to think fast and grabbed a table to roll in front of the destroyed door, then a chair, and another.

Everyone in the club was still down low, fearfully wailing at the sounds of growling and slamming bodies inside. Blake grabbed the chubby bouncer by the arm, pulled him, and parked him on his ass in front of the upturned table barricade, then searched the room for anyone who wasn't panicking in case there was more trouble. Loud, vicious barking echoed and snarling and bones breaking with sickening snaps could be heard. Then one last slam of what sounded like a gunny sack smashing a window followed a long, low growl that ended the fight.

It was over, but now Blake held his breath at the uncomfortable silence within the barricaded room. Beaded sweat rolled down his neck. He readied his 12-gauge short barrel, tried for a peek into the room, and saw Simon bathed in blood, pulling his coat back onto his human form. He watched still as Simon lifted the blonde girl from the floor delicately. With a better look, Blake took in the sight of the carnage with a familiar disgust. The leather couches were broken and upturned. There were streams of red below impact splatters on the walls, and the two male bodies were lying in thick pools on the floor under them. The head of one had been removed and was not in plain sight. The other lay on his back, surrounded by shattered glass from the table against the far wall.

"Move that damned thing," Simon grunted as he adjusted the girl in his arms. "This one's just knocked out. Get me an address. The other's not breathing and needs to get to a hospital." As soon as they started rolling the table aside, he was out the VIP door with Angel in his arms and she only in her knee-high boots. Simon left wet, red bootprints behind.

One of the girls rushed forward, pulling a bouncer's oversized jacket around herself, close enough to whisper. "I picked the girls up for coffee a few weeks ago. They're over on Cyprus. It's a second-floor apartment with an ugly green door. Like, maybe a block from the Fletcher Library."

Simon grunted and shifted the blonde in his arms, and kicked the exit door open to leave.

Blake had to steady himself quickly, then ignored the gore in the room as he rushed in to get Rose out. Her limp body was slippery in his arms. She had been sprayed with blood, and her face was streaked with more of it. Blake came back out of the room quickly and turned to his bouncers, who had finally grouped up to see what they could do. Their bodies lined up to shield the public from seeing the girl he carried.

Shouting through the music still playing, he announced, "Alright, boys, get everybody out of here. Close off that room. No pictures! Got it?"

Blake turned to another of the men, this one tall and dark-skinned, and transferred the girl over to him. "Geoff, take her to the ER. Tell them you didn't see what happened." He flipped a couple of switches on the wall nearby, and the white lights came up, and the music cut out. "You all deaf? Everybody out, I said! We're closed!"

He made sure Geoff got out first without any problems. The black bouncer's drop-top silver coupe left the parking lot flinging gravel. Blake turned next to the door with his gun pointed down at his side and watched for the panicked patrons to get in their cars to leave. A short moment passed with the crowd still milling through the entrance. He heard squealing tires, smashing glass, and car horns blowing a few blocks away.

Blake followed the sound with his eyes, unable to see the source. "Christ's sake! Now what?"

Blake tucked the shotgun into the saddle bag of his bike and struggled with the key in his tight jeans pocket. He flipped the key and twisted the steer hard as he walked it back out of its space to drive out of the lot. The throttle opened, and his motorcycle engine bit and growled at the night as he made his second lean through a yellow light that was turning. As he pulled around the bend toward the inner city, he squeezed the brake hard and screeched to a fish-tailing stop. Right after the turn, the car he was looking for had crossed traffic into the front of a pizzeria. The picnic tables outside were broken through and flung about, and the silver-colored coupe was smashed into the brick face of the building. The passenger door was left open, and the horn was blasting relentlessly. Black and white smoke rolled out from under the crushed hood, and a fire had started. Another car had skidded to a stop before colliding and another behind it. The accident caught the attention of a few nearby pedestrians.

Blake flung out the kickstand on his bike and ran to the car, yelling for everyone to stay back. Through the window, he saw the girl was gone, and the tall bouncer lay limp across the wheel. He pulled him back to find blood and a lot of it coming from his neck and shoulder, which had been torn open, much worse than his own was years ago. Geoff was struggling to breathe. Blake ripped the door open, reached across the driver to hook under his arms, and pulled just as the fire blew out of the console, shunting the stereo and console controls out dangerously close to Blake's face. He swore loudly as he tugged again, freeing the larger man's limp body and dragging him away from the burning vehicle.

Once they were on the opposite side of the street, Blake

looked up to see a line of stopped cars and several more people watching. Bleating sirens and wailing of the firehouse horn from a block away broke the commotion as the blaze took over the car's interior and blackened some of the brick against it. The burly black bouncer in Blake's clutches gurgled, sputtered, and then stopped moving as life left him. There was no sign of Rose except one of her red high-heeled shoes on the ground just outside the car.

A Valiant Effort

Melissa ran from the wreckage as if on fawn legs. She looked curiously at her blood-soaked and unreasonably steady hands, then felt over her still-naked chest, looking for a thumping heartbeat. She was quite taken aback that it wasn't drowning out the sirens that rushed to the victim she'd left behind or pounding in her head due to the collision. She pulled the ends of her Kool-aid red hair from the corner of her mouth and ran off in the opposite direction of the noise. In the middle of the block, she stopped just out of light to find a shiny black stretch limousine carefully parking directly in her path. As she stood waiting in the shadows, the driver casually walked to open the rear door facing her direction.

The man was a little taller than she, with a crooked but genuine, small smile. He wore a pressed, double-breasted black driver's coat and matching cadet-style hat like in an old movie. He gestured to her and then the door and after a short pause, spoke out.

"Come then, miss. We mustn't dilly dally. Morning comes too soon, I'm afraid," he warned.

The chauffeur spoke with a slight accent. It was very proper, New England, perhaps. Melissa emerged slowly from the shadows and looked to either side of what must be the quietest street in the city at that hour. As soon as the light caught her still unclothed body, the man quickly unbuttoned and stripped off his coat and readied it to wrap around her.

When she saw his offer, she rushed to him and allowed herself to step into its broad shoulders without slipping into the sleeves he straightened and wrapped around her. She pulled her arms together inside and held the coat closed by the lapels as she stepped into the back seat of the car where he had indicated.

A few seconds after her door clicked closed, the car began to glide away. She sat in a luxurious space suited for holding a small party. The leather seats were quite large and in pristine condition. Above her, a tinted moon roof showed passing street lights, and a telephone clung just inside the door whose sleek tan color matched the leather. A wet bar lined one side, while a long bench seat with an accompanying tinted window occupied the other. Suitable small rope lighting dimly lit the cabin and reflected off various drinking glasses hanging to her left. A privacy partition was in place, blocking her view of the driver or the road ahead. It seemed as soon as she'd taken in her surroundings, they had come to a full stop, and her door was opening again.

"Please pardon my not bringing you to the front door, miss," the driver apologized. "I was certain you'd prefer to clean yourself and change clothes before being introduced."

She was still trying to sort out her situation when she asked, "Hey, who are you anyway? What do you want with me?"

"Questions later, miss," he politely chided. "Proceed into the door there, and straight upstairs to the left, you'll find a place to bathe. The rest of your needs have been arranged."

He held the door for her patiently and then clicked it closed again after she stepped out. When she tried to offer his coat back, he simply held up a hand with his same smile and directed her with a nod to the large estate she hadn't yet noticed. Melissa hesitated outside the mansion, with its colonial-style columns and immaculate brick build. An intercom was situated at a security gate, presumably linked to another near the broad, white back door. Before a button could be pressed, the obscured, barred steel gate glided open to one side. Inside stood two girls she recognized from the club, now in casual blouses and jeans but still in heavy makeup with their hair down. Melissa identified Kitty, a short, brunette woman with a round face and girlish dimples, and Dusty, a ginger-haired thirty-something with long runway features. They stood out, not belonging in a place like this.

Both leaned on clasped hands affixed to the left hip like staged dolls. Melissa looked at them both with hair-raised tension, like she was looking at something she'd never seen before that wasn't meant to exist. The tight strain set her posture on a defensive edge. She pulled an unapproving sneer across her smudged lips as she stood still and awaited some move or explanation.

"Well then," Dusty began in a low, southern accent that rolled from her lips like honey. She loosed her interlocked fingers, shifted to balance her anaconda legs, and continued, "Now that you've found your way here to Valiant, we gotta get you cleaned up and into some proper clothes." She gestured toward the mansion behind her as if she were a game show valet presenting a new puzzle.

The soft-bodied brunette, with a non-too-prominent mole just left of her upturned nose, lifted a covered box by a handle on top. The box seemed large enough to need two hands, depending on the weight of its contents, but it seemed to carry as easily for Kitty as an awkwardly shaped clutch purse. The women led Melissa inside toward a staircase that curled against the plastered wall to a dark, carpeted hallway. Every footstep absorbed into an eerie silence as Melissa followed them like their steps were weightless. She pushed blood-crusted stray hairs behind her ear out of her face.

Dusty propped open a broad door with a brass handle and flicked on a light to reveal a lavish bathroom. "Clean up in here; take your time," she began and gestured with a long finger. "When you're done, your room is just three doors down."

Kitty stepped into the room indicated and reemerged without the crate, then they walked down the hall away from her without further words.

Once the other women left her sight, Melissa's bound-up feeling left her body, and she calmed considerably as she stepped across the cool tile. She approached the sink and looked into the mirror to see an unoccupied room. She turned, looked to be certain the room behind her matched the image in the glass and turned back. Melissa touched her face with the dried blood on her hands the way a child might smear finger paints, as though it would make her appear as the coarse, dry flakes clung to her cheeks. And yet the glass before her would show none of her efforts. She rubbed it into her skin until it was cracked and raw, digging her nails into her flesh, hoping to see fresh blood drip from the void in the reflection. But nothing had changed. Looking down, she stopped and watched the tiny blood drops gently strike the clean, white porcelain as they made skinny wiggling legs down the curved basin toward the drain.

She studied the blood streaks with careful eyes. She awaited the tangle of confused emotions to flood her chest with a tightening ache that never twisted within her. She tried to cry and made her body shudder inwardly as she did so, though still, nothing but frustration came to furrow her brow and stretch her lips for unformed words. Not a single tear would well or fall. The scratches she'd made on herself had burned slightly, but the heat of pain had already subsided. When she touched her face again with delicate fingers, the scratches were gone, and she felt herself grow weak. Her belly and throat seemed to be trying to wring themselves as hunger crept over her.

Melissa stepped into the tub and cranked the hot valve wide open. She let the water spray over her while standing there and holding herself. The water flowed over her lips but had no taste. Either the water was scalding, or her skin was freezing. The steam reaction revealed it could be both. The shower streams stung and cascaded down to her feet, where the water tinted pink and swirled away down the drain between her painted toes. She stared thunderstruck at the smudged red faucet handle as the drain swallowed the runoff. With no account of how much time had passed, Melissa turned off the water and pulled on a fluffy white terrycloth robe before finding her way to the room indicated as hers. The closet door was open, revealing a full rack of varied clothing. After closer inspection, the outfits and shoes matched her own sizes.

"Sure am glad that's not creepy at all," she said just above a whisper. The sarcasm in her monologue was meant for no one, but her shoulders relaxed as if someone else put her at ease.

Her words seemed to illicit a reaction from the crate Kitty had left behind. The sound of discontent mewling could be heard from inside it on the floor. Melissa approached one step at a time, her toes curling like they were gripping the hardwood as she approached. She finally reached and loosed the hook on the crate and pulled the door open. After a shallow hiss from inside, a gangly-looking cat ran out and backed itself into a corner of the room opposite her as she squared to close the distance.

Melissa's tongue twitched rhythmically. It ticked like a clock. Faster and faster against the backs of her protruding, sharp teeth as she prowled closer. The cat drew itself up and hissed loudly, ready to attack. Her hands were fast and caught the limber tabby as it leaped at her, but the breaking of its neck had slowed the incessant ticking of her tongue in time with its heartbeat. Her arms trickled with blood from the cat's claw swipe, and she sank her teeth into the neck to drink while it was still warm.

Under His Wing

Tanya inhaled sharply, taking in the smells of leather and chocolate as she finally regained consciousness. Her left cheekbone throbbed almost as much as the back of her head. She opened her eyes to a blurry, soft light, but her sudden motion of sitting up made the room spin and her stomach lurch. Her face screwed in anguish as she reached behind her to the source of pain where her fingers touched her matted-dry and tangled hair above her neck, and she could feel a thin wadded bandage taped into place.

When she opened her eyes again, she could follow the leather smell belonging to a rather large coat wrapped around her. Tanya's only other clothing was her costume thong, making her quickly aware that nothing she remembered was a dream. She grabbed the lapels and pulled the coat open slightly to see that on her left side, under her breast, was a stain of pink that contrasted her delicate, light skin tone. It was blood, but she thought it couldn't be her own.

A sort of rhythmic scraping and jingling sound from her kitchen caused her to quickly pull the coat tight around her. She pulled her knees up to her chest and scooted back into the corner of the couch. She gasped out loud when her eyes landed on the apartment door, which was still slightly open, the jamb having been broken. Just then, a tall, brawny man came around the corner stirring something in his hands. The light from the kitchen caught his wavy, long brown-grey hair, casting a shadow across his face.

She screamed.

Tanya closed her eyes tightly, shaking her head as she tried to lift her arms in front of her. Her hands gnarled up before her eyes, as a last defense as they froze in place. She gently slumped as the tension subsided from the severe clenching. Tanya's eyes opened to the man's brutish form drawing nearer, with a hand out toward her, and he tried to shush her.

"Don't move," the strange man said. "It'll only hurt more."

She loosed another tight-lipped, pathetic wail, and tears pooled in her eyes as her arms flailed about desperately. She pushed off the couch and out of the trapping, heavy leather coat to try to run and only collapsed on feeble legs.

"Wake up," he said. "Come on, you've got to stay conscious if you're gonna get better."

The stranger in her apartment watched as she stirred and blinked back with watering, sea-green eyes. "Hey, there you are," he said, attempting a soothing tone.

"Who... Who the hell are you?" Tanya half-whispered in accusation as she looked about the room.

Thin tears openly streamed and blackened from the running makeup around her eyes when she noticed splinters on the floor near her broken door. She could see the man waiting patiently. He watched her take in the damage until her eyes returned to him. His face was framed with dangling uncombed sandy hair, and he was at least a couple of days without a shave. She caught herself staring when she reached his steely unwavering eyes. He sat on the edge of the couch next to her and cast a shadow over her from the kitchen light behind him. Her lip trembled, and she flinched again with a scrunched expression.

"Don't move too much," he said to her with a warning. "I'm Simon. I'm a friend." He picked up the mug, offered it to her handle first, and said, "Drink this. You'll feel better, and it might help to keep you awake."

When she took the cup, he moved closer to reach around behind her and knelt to look more closely at the back of her head. His large hands made delicate work of pulling aside her hair and removing the bandage. Simon gently pressed near the wound. Tanya held still, albeit with a shaky breath that fluttered from her loose bottom lip. She tensed immediately at his touch, placing both hands around the mug. The aroma of the hot cocoa was weak but clear and present.

"You're safe," he continued. "You should try to shower when you feel up to it. When you do, make sure to put on a clean dressing for this," he indicated with another pressing of his warm fingers. "It looks like the bleeding has stopped."

"That really hurts," she cried quietly. She twitched a little at his touch but held still and tightly shut her eyes in a grimace.

"If you think you need to go to a doc, I can take you," Simon said. "Do you remember anything? How you got hurt?" he asked, moving to sit on the edge of a small coffee table off-centered in front of the couch.

"Where's Missy? Is... is she alright?" Tanya asked between sniffling.

Simon looked steadily into her face when she could keep her eyes open to see him. He kept steady eye contact but only offered, "She's in good hands."

"What does that mean? Who were those guys?" she rattled, each question getting slightly louder, more frantic, and recoiled painfully between each of these outbursts.

He stood silently, waiting for her to calm down, but his face showed no emotion as he held his tongue.

She sat up with her feet on the floor and tried clumsily to stand. "I... I don't want to be alone," she said.

Simon placed a heavy, warm hand on her shoulder before she could rise. "You rest. Finish drinking that and keep your head up," he said. "Those guys will no longer be a problem."

She wavered and struggled, which made even small actions difficult. The room was off balance and out of focus. He lifted her chin with a finger and, with the other hand, helped her bring the steaming mug back close to her lips.

He looked into her eyes and repeated, "Drink it all. Do you feel tired? Like you'll have trouble staying awake?"

Tanya took a little drink. "No," she said, "it just stings. I don't remember much. We were doing a private show for those guys. Kind of a sister act thing, ya know? And," she stifled a sob to continue, "the other guy had his hands all over Missy, which he's not supposed to do, but when they're dressed like that, you can make some extra cash if you let 'em touch and stuff."

She took a long drink then and tipped the mug up to finish the cocoa but refused the unmixed sludge that remained in the bottom. Simon took the nearly empty cup to place it on the table as she wiped her lips with the back of her hand and swallowed hard.

Her eyes rolled up and over as the large gulp finally passed through, and she continued. "Then he... He wouldn't let go of her, and he bit her... like on her throat. I might not have noticed 'cause Missy was busy with the other guy, you know? But she moaned or something, and it made me look up, and then my guy grabbed me too, all of the sudden like he was gonna do the same thing, and I screamed."

Simon maintained his stoic, unflinching expression as he listened, suppressing any emotion he may have. His presence remained the only sign of concern.

"He pushed me down and tried to force himself on me when I heard the door slam. Then," she choked out, crying into her hands, "the lights went out."

Simon let her cry without saying a word, then took the cup and stood to go and rinse it in the sink. When he returned to her a minute later, she stood again, but slowly this time, with his long coat still wrapped around her.

"I better take that shower. Then I need to use your phone to call the hospital to see if Missy is there," she said.

She made her way carefully down the hall to the bathroom and hung his coat on the outside doorknob before closing it.

Simon took a few minutes to inspect the damage he had done breaking in the apartment door. He went to the jeep to fetch a few things to make it at least close out the cold until he could properly fix it. When he was done forcing a few new screw holes and rigging the latch, he dialed Blake to find out about the other girl.

"Hey," Simon started, "Did you take care of the girl?" As he listened to Blake recount the crash and make his excuses of her fleeing, he angrily cut him off with a whispered shout. "Dammit! I told you to take care of her," Simon seethed in frustration and ground his teeth between Blake's attempts to explain. Simon broke in, not letting Blake finish speaking. "Find the girl. This one's already asking questions. She wasn't bitten, but she saw everything. If you can save her, fine. If not..." he looked up at the closed bedroom door. "If not, finish it. Just handle it."

Simon ended the call and waked his tools out to the jeep. He returned to the apartment to the sweet smells of vanilla and cranberry with a subtle linger of pipe water. The blonde woman came into view wrapped with a large, flowery pink towel and returned to Simon in her living room.

She pulled her hair to one side over her shoulder and asked, "Do you have any more of those bandages? We only have little, finger-sized ones."

"Yeah, in my jeep," Simon answered. "In the morning, we should get you some more and supplies to fix your door. Maybe even some food. You've barely got a scrap in the place."

Perks of Management

When he returned to the Rougir de Vie, Blake contemplated beginning the cleanup of the night's fiasco. He dismounted his Harley, threw out the rest of his cigarette, and then went inside to find that a couple of the girls and one of his bouncers were waiting for him. Blake brushed his knuckles across the underside of his jaw where his stubble was always a bit more coarse over old fingernail scars.

A tall, fit bouncer uncrossed his arms and stood away from the bar where he was leaning to approach Blake as he entered the main floor room. "You wanna tell me what that was all about?" he asked, furrowing one brow as the other cocked upward.

"Look, Brandt," Blake started with a shrug, "it was a bad, bad night. Has anyone called the police about this?"

Folding his arms again, Brandt nodded his head toward the girls. "They're worried about working tomorrow, so I ain't called anybody."

"Leave it at that, then," he ordered. "We better start the cleanup if we intend to open again. I don't want this place turning into a crime scene."

The bouncer's arms flew out in surprise. "Are you kiddin' me, boss? Two men are dead. We can't just let it be!"

"I said, leave it. They got theirs for the trouble they caused. I'll handle it if anyone comes asking." Blake was fuming with the entire situation. "Just go home and get some rest. This is my mess. I'll clean it up," Blake added. "I want to get started before it gets too late."

Brandt reached over the bar to grab his jacket, shaking his head. "You're the boss," he said, submitting. "Call me if we're up and running tomorrow." He made his way past Blake and pushed the door open to leave.

"What about us?" came the syrupy voice of an overly slim dancer girl with blue-green hair. Long, orange fingernails gently dragged over Blake's back, which caused him to turn and face the two girls who were still waiting. "We don't all have somewhere to go, and if we close…." The one speaking brought her icy hands up over his pecs, eliciting a shudder. "How's a couple of girls supposed to eat?"

Blake watched her in a hypnotic fix as she curled her upper lip to bare a long, sharp incisor, which she tickled with the tip of her tongue. She pressed her body against his growing arousal. Blake bent, scooped up the tiny woman at her waist, and bent her over one shoulder. He carried her toward the other waiting dancer with black hair and neon green tips. He lifted her the same way over his other shoulder and carried them with kicking feet and laughter toward the dressing room area.

"I'll take care of tonight as best I can," he said. "You just worry about tomorrow."

Blake emerged several hours later from the hallway which connected the gentlemen's club to a small apartment row in the back of the building. He pulled on a simple, black t-shirt and rested each foot on a stool rung to tighten his boot laces. He glanced above the bar at the clock's harsh red numbers reading just shy of four o'clock. With a heavy huff, he steadied himself against the bar and, after a long dizzy moment, reached under the bar sink for what remained of a bottle of bleach and several heavy, black waste can liners.

After tying a clean blue paisley bandana into place over his hair, he set quickly to work, then pulled on some too-tight latex gloves. Blake reluctantly opened the door and found the wait had only festered the mess and remains. His face corked and twisted with an expression of disgust. Blake loudly reminded himself, "Breathe through your mouth and just keep moving." He chuffed with a shake of his head. "Perks of management."

He pressed his dried lips together and set to work in a dizzy, drained stupor. Blake carefully searched the pockets of both men, garnering cell phones, wallets, loose change, a wristwatch, a few rings, and a book of matches bearing the logo of a place called "Shadow Puppets."

"What the hell are they doing out here?" he asked out loud in disbelief.

He pocketed the matches, IDs, and cash from the wallets and took a moment to access each of the flip phones for any leads. A list of recent calls was available, but no relevant text exchanges. Noting the handful of recent calls to the same number, the most recent of which occurred just before the night's events, to a number simply labeled "Lady Cleo." Blake entered the number into his phone with the same name, hoping it could get him some answers.

Blake then went to work, pushing out what little furniture there was to make room to properly clean the space. He was about to put the heavy plastic bags to use when he stopped to notice the club's owner, Michael, standing in the doorway. Michael pushed a handful of slender fingers through his sleek rain of black hair and let it fall as he stepped inside the room.

"I don't think this kind of party is what I had in mind for this room when I opened the place," Michael said with an almost dormant French accent. He looked over the damage with a plastic grin. Long vertical laugh lines deepened at either side of his face to barrier his black pencil mustache. "We did agree that with the sort of employ we carry that there may be some occupational hazards."

Blake stood and nodded, "Yeah, I'm just not used to this shit being so close to home. Mind lending a hand?" he asked, hopefully.

"Don't worry about it," Michael waved. "You've already put in a full night, and I just got in. I'll handle it." He smoothed his hair back with both hands and pushed up the sleeves of his plaid button shirt, and added, "Why don't you take a few days off? Let me put some money into this room, and set up some mailers for the patrons who had to cut their party short?"

"You sure?" Blake asked in disbelief, dropping his chin when he heard Michael offer to do work.

Michael nodded again as though reading his employee's thoughts. "I got this," he assured his general manager. "Here's my card for your expenses," he said, pulling a credit card from his wallet. "Consider it a gift for my absence during a difficult situation that I feel you handled quite well."

Blake took the card and stepped past his partner, then went to drop his clothes into the washing machine. He started running a steaming shower noting that both he and those articles needed a good hot soak. His phone chirped a notification from the ledge on the sink that he decided could wait as he climbed in under the pathetic, soft jets of water. Once he had finished and dried, he read the message from Dusty.

"Rose is gonna bunk at my place for a few nights. Can't let a hungry girl out in the cold all alone."

"Aw, Christ!" He barked at the screen. "That's just great."

The sun was peeking through a wisp of clouds when Blake finally went outside to light a smoke, wearing nothing but lounge pants tied loosely at the waist despite the November morning chill. He dragged deeply on a freshly lit smoke like it was the last one he may ever have. He pulled deeply on his cigarette and gagged, looking toward the roof as the wind carried a fetid odor under his nose. He flicked the remainder of his cigarette away and spat hard to dislodge the unforgettable new taste.

"I guess up there is about as good a place as any," Blake muttered as he held his belly and his breath. He returned inside to the bed where he'd left both dancers to find they had left the bed empty but just as cold as when they were in it with him.

Contact Solutions

Tanya made Simon keep his promise to take her to the hospital again early. Afterward, he took her to retrieve some things to fix the door. She also talked him into calling Blake until he woke up to open the club so she could retrieve her phone and purse. She left Melissa's things in case she came back there first to look for them. They picked up some medicine and bandages for the wound that already seemed to no longer bother her.

She was surprised at how quickly Simon set to work when they returned to her apartment. He cut out the splintered section on the door frame where the damage had been done, making as little mess as possible with the simple hand tools he'd brought.

"I don't understand why I haven't heard anything from her yet. And if she's not at the hospital, where could she be?" Tanya asked, showing her frustration and worry again as she had all morning.

As he had most of the morning, Simon kept silent to her questions and worries. At most, he would offer her a shrug or a sympathetic smile.

Tanya left him alone to work after he ignored her and went into the bathroom to medicate the wound under her hair and redress it. She had carefully styled her hair so it wouldn't show, straightening her feathery locks to frame her face. She

couldn't help but notice as she returned to the living room
how he carefully cut and measured the pieces for her door
without any electrical tools whatsoever.

She paced between rooms after she unpacked her bag from
the pharmacy and put the leftover items away. She watched
him work through the fitting, cleared her throat, and lingered
closely as if he might notice her there at one time. With as
much presence and whimper as she could muster whenever
he looked her way, she folded her arms, raised an eyebrow, or
rested a hand on her hip, always taking a breath as if to speak
before the sounds of his work would stop her short.

"Very old-fashioned," she said aloud, once, not even sure
she had meant to do so. Tanya hesitated a moment after she
spoke and gave Simon time for a response even though he
again said nothing.

Simon only turned and smiled, and after sizing the new piece
of molded trim against the jamb, he sanded the edges smooth
to fit it snugly into the space.

"Well, you are pretty handy, though, aren't you?" Tanya
complimented.

Simon nodded with a forced smile as he finished screwing
the knob tightly into place, more at the job finished than
responding to her rhetoric. "Just something my father taught
me," he said, finally. "It's all set. Good as new." He tested
the tension of the knob and the fit into the frame with the
weather seal.

"Alright, how do you want to kill some time?" Tanya asked. "'Cause I need something else to think about, or I'll go nuts."

"I'll try to reach Blake again," Simon answered. "Maybe he's heard something."

As he reached for his out-of-date flip phone, he looked twice at the screen and urgently thumbed a few buttons. Tanya audibly gruffed and returned to the kitchen, where she'd drawn a tub of soapy water for the handful of dishes still soaking in the sink. As her hands reached down to dive into the bubbles, Simon spoke a few feet behind her, which made her jump with rolling eyes at how easy it was for him to go undetected.

"Got a call from Blake," he said with displeasure in his voice. "He says Rose, er, I mean Melissa, hasn't been in touch."

She squeezed her eyes tightly closed and flicked the soapy water off her fingers. Her sight was blurred and wet at the edges when she turned to face Simon, crossing her arms to lean back against the counter.

"So," Tanya managed, making her lips curl and part as though words would form themselves. Then after a quiet moment, she asked, "So should we go looking for her? Maybe try the," her voice broke, and she drew a difficult breath. "Try the hospital again?"

Simon's eyes looked between hers as if he might find the answer she wanted in doing so. He gave up with a long blink and answered, "If you'd like to, I won't deny you. But I need to take care of some other things. I'll take you back to get your car," he offered. Simon left the room to pack his tools and clean his mess of sawdust and extra pieces from the door fix.

Much of the useful part of the day had been spent gathering supplies and working. By the time they approached the inner city, the sun had peeked through the streets and shone final reflections off the glass of tall buildings, blinding out sign letterings. Just before they reached the parking lot for the club, the purple sky showed a glimpse of stars. Tanya was distracted, looking up to avoid the awkward silence in the car, when her phone chimed.

She wrestled with her bag to retrieve her phone, and the banner on her screen showed a notification that read, "New message from Blake Gentry." Tanya quickly unlocked the screen to open it.

The message read, "Hey, your sister hasn't been in to pick up her stuff. Thought you'd like to know. Hope you're doing okay. The club is closed until we get cleaned up."

With a raging, closed-mouth scream and a jutting of her lower teeth, Tanya threw her head back and grasped the phone tightly. It vibrated before she could reopen her eyes, and a tune began to play. She turned it to face her and saw an unassigned number.

As Simon parked the jeep, she answered as calmly and politely as possible. "Hello...?"

"Hey Tilly," Melissa spoke dearly into the borrowed phone, using Tanya's nickname. "No, I'm fine. Well, not fine. I just woke up." She paused as a mix of angry and joyful chatter loudly came back through the speaker. "It's Kitty's phone. She must've brought me to her place last night after," she waited as Tanya cut her off with more questions. "No, I'll be home tonight, but I'm gonna skip work, okay? Still pretty dizzy. No, don't come to get me. I'll be fine," she waited as Tanya argued to make her excuse. "I just need to take it easy, so I'm gonna lay back down and stay here for a while, okay? Alright, I love you too. See you soon."

Melissa pressed the End button on the screen and returned it to Kitty. She stood and took a few steps, then turned back to Kitty and Dusty, who stayed to see how the call went.

"Will the hunger pass?" she asked, running her fingers over her belly and uncomfortably up her arms as they crossed.

Kitty fixed her gaze on the preoccupied fledgling Melissa and replied evenly, "You already know the answer. You have to feed your hunger. You'll have to learn to hunt."

Melissa pulled at the bottom hem on her rumpled shirt that had twisted at her waist, then pushed her dangling, dark hair back over her left ear. Her hair was freshly washed clean of the bright red dye earlier as she tried to regain her sense of self, and it lay partially wet and twisted across her shoulder. "You mean more strays, like the one you left here for me?" she asked hopefully.

Dusty looked up at her from her seat at the vanity on a matching, unupholstered, straight-backed chair with her long legs crossed at rest. "I think you already know that can't last, honey," she said with a hint of warning. "Soon, it simply won't be enough. Your hunger will tell you what it needs." She pursed her painted, glittery pink lips, kissed the air in Melissa's direction, and then stood to leave. "But now that you've decided to stay in for the night, we'd better get going. Mr. Gentry said the club is closed for remodeling, so we're off to do some hunting of our own."

Kitty leaned toward the tri-fold vanity mirror, where Melissa saw only the drapes and sconce on the wall behind herself and the large, empty bed across the room. As Kitty raised her hands over her shoulders, the ringlets of her mahogany curls suddenly reflected. As did her cherubic round face, upon which she reapplied a bit of foundation from a tiny drawer to cover a few peeking freckles. Long, sunrise lashes flared out around Kitty's green eyes, and she winked with a teasing smile before the reflection wavered away. Again, only the room, its furniture, and light fixtures remained in view in the looking glass. Kitty laughed as Melissa looked at her with confused awe, then followed Dusty out the door, taking her purse from its hanging place on the knob. The odd pair strode into the hallway without closing the door behind them.

Staking Her Claim

When Melissa woke in the manor guest bedroom, the gentleman driver stood waiting outside the open door with a robe draped over one arm. She sat up and pushed strands of hair back from her face that was stuck near her lips. She opened her eyes to the sight of dry blood and colored fur stuck to her fingers for the second night in a row and looked at the house servant with questions she could not utter. In response to her mouth trying to form words, he opened the robe and nodded to her with a long, understanding blink as he waited for Melissa to go to him.

"I'm afraid you may need another bath, miss. Such is the trouble of choosing to feed as you have been," he said apologetically. "But we'd be remiss to meet the master of the house in such a disheveled state."

Melissa peeked through the shower's steam several times to see the older man still standing there, turned to one side as if waiting to serve her every need. He had left her alone once for a moment, brought back a folded garment to hang just outside the door, and placed a pair of delicate flat dress slippers on the floor under it. She took her time, scrubbing her face over and over more aggressively each time as if she still felt unclean. She finally turned the water off and left the melting bar of soap on the floor of the tub, where she dropped it in frustration.

The gentleman held open a thick towel as he looked away for

her to step in to dry. He finally took the time to introduce himself as the manor's primary servant. "You may address me as Thaddeus, miss."

Once Melissa had the towel wrapped in place, he went to fetch the dress and slippers without so much as a word or even a heavy breath of impatience. His hands were careful to barely make any contact as if it were forbidden while he helped her zip into her simple black dress. Lastly, he presented the slippers and placed them conveniently for her to step into them.

"I do hope you won't find this outfit in poor taste, miss." Thaddeus said. "I had guessed heeled shoes would be inappropriate while getting your bearings. And, of course, a color fit for mourning the life behind you now, but simple and comfortable enough to have a proper walk about the estate so you might become more familiar with your new home, should you choose to stay with us."

The steps in the foyer were carved from marble and held the curve of the portrait-adorned wall into the main hall. Thaddeus made his arm available for her to grasp on the way. She refused it, choosing instead to let her hand glide down the glossy hardwood railing opposite the man.

"We'll go into the cellar first, as you're sure to need access to our estate reserve more so than other libations the house might offer," Thaddeus explained. "I am not particularly fond of capturing and tending to strays. However, if you deem it necessary, of course, I will be happy to oblige your needs."

With his polite guidance, they found an ornate door to another set of less-than-elegant stairs to descend into a much cooler, darker area. At the bottom of the stairs, Thaddeus took a lantern from a support post nail and lit a match to give fire to the oil-soaked cotton wick.

He gave a grin in the fire's light and looked between the young woman's face and the lantern. "We attempted to modernize some of the estate's features like this one, but I found replacing fuses and batteries to be quite unpleasant compared to old-fashioned oil, and the light is a bit more reliable even if not as bright." He stepped forward, offering his arm again, which Melissa took this time, even though the floor was quite sturdy and level. "What you see here tonight is not meant to alarm you. This is merely an effective means of harvest for the master and his children, and often the least complicated."

Just as the servant's words became lost in the dark, Melissa caught sight of another person in the cellar with them. A young man, with his arms suspended by his wrists out at his sides and stripped of any upper body clothing. His squinting, pained expression was that of someone who hadn't recently seen any light. The bound man squeezed his eyes shut when the lantern came close.

"Now, child, we do not forbid feeding directly from our guests," Thaddeus went on softly. "However, we prefer a much more modern, sustainable method of procuring our needful things with as little harm as required."

With that, he stood the lantern on a nearby tray table, carefully arranged with surgical instruments and a group of glass juice carafes. Thaddeus took up a box of latex gloves from a shelf underneath and offered them to Melissa. She shook her head and stepped back wordlessly.

He replaced the box on the shelf and looked at her directly. "You won't always be able to ignore the hunger inside you, miss," he said. "And as we go to meet Master Fletcher, you'll find you'd have rather been sated beforehand. But that choice is your own, of course. For now. It is not wise to let your thirst rule your decisions." He paused momentarily and lifted the lantern, again offering his arm to her. "Shall we retire to the upstairs? Or would you prefer some time here to change your mind?"

Again, Melissa shook her head, but more slowly and unsure this time, with a hand over her belly as if trying to stifle the temptation of the offered blood. She looked over her shoulder, searching aimlessly in the dark for the stairs to the exit, and looked back to the manor's servant, who was again waiting patiently.

"I think it might be better to come back later," Melissa said, not daring to outright refuse. "The thought of meeting your Mr. Fletcher sounds more…appetizing." Her tone carried like a sale, the way she might with one of her club customers.

Thaddeus leaned close with the lantern glow under his face, highlighting his gaunt, desolate features. "Young lady," he said with a warning and low voice. "You are free to deny what you are to the brink of its dangers. But keep in mind I do not bear that same luxury."

A quiet jingling interrupted them in the darkness. Thaddeus retrieved a small cellular phone from his inner jacket pocket. The screen light illuminated his face in a pale blue as he quickly scanned the message.

"Our meeting must be postponed," he said, returning the device behind his jacket breast. "Mr. Fletcher has some urgent business to attend to." His more nurturing expression returned from the serious age-lined face that was too close a moment before. "Let's get you upstairs, miss. There is much more to explore while we have this time to ourselves."

Blake ended a call, rechecked his directions, and threw a leg over his motorcycle. He took a moment to close all the open windows on his newly purchased smartphone's screen and returned it to his breast pocket. He took another glance at his sleek, side-shaved haircut, with a tight braid of long hair he couldn't part with, and then strapped on a helmet that he usually didn't wear on shorter trips. The helmet was emblazoned with twin anacondas around the crown. Their large green mouths opened toward the visor against a gunmetal gray background. He twisted the throttle and leaned his bike away from the failing light of the city sunset toward the busier district, hoping to arrive just before this club called Shadow Puppets might be opening for the night.

As he traveled through this unfamiliar part of his sister city, he leisurely cruised down the empty streets, killing time instead of thundering down each of them in a hurry as he might on familiar turf. Lights were shining through broad clean windows where some clerks or bureaucrats might be working late in a downtown court building. A little diner around the corner had a sign on the sidewalk boasting a homemade chili on special where the street light above flicked on as Blake rode by. Several street lights nearing the south side of town were visibly broken and stood unhelpful in districts like these, where the roads could also use a little attention from the city's budget. Lane lines were unpainted, and graffiti adorned several buildings' outer walls and under railroad bridges. He noticed some people wandering the street who appeared homeless or, at least, down on their luck judging by their tattered clothing and lack of hygiene as they stood outside in groups near abandoned buildings.

A disheveled little convenience store was ahead with a letter missing from its blinking OPEN sign. He let off the throttle and pulled up to a pump to fill up for the ride home later. Blake stretched his legs, carried in his helmet, and looked at the glass wall of refrigerated products just long enough for the obnoxious bells to ring above the shop entrance. He plucked an energy drink from the sparsely stocked rack and let the door clap shut on its beaten, worn-out gasket. The young man who had just entered looked toward him, following the clapping sound. Blake watched in the filthy glass door reflection as the new customer shoved his hands deep into his pockets and lowered his eyes. He was shorter by nearly a head and wore a closed, oversized flannel button-down. He could barely see the young man had a small patch of wiry chin hair under his sweaty upper lip on brown skin.

Blake sidled past the Hispanic customer excusing himself, picked up a nutty candy bar on the way to the counter, and checked his vest pocket to see he was down to three cigarettes. "Put five on your second pump and a pack of short reds," he said, pointing lazily over the squatty, tired-looking, full-bearded Indian clerk to the top rack at his brand. As he reached for his wallet to start choosing the bills for his total, he felt something rigid press against his ribs from his side.

"Put your wallet and your hands on the counter, asshole," the young man demanded through his teeth. "And you!" he indicated to the clerk. "Empty the drawer in a bag, or you and this gringo gonna get bloody." He lifted the gun to Blake's cheek and twisted the cold steel barrel.

Blake did as instructed, for the moment, pushing his drink to the side closer to the gunman as he placed his hands calmly in sight. He looked out of the corner of his eye at the curly-haired gunman. He was sweating from his brow and wide-eyed.

"Tell ya what, kid. There's three hundred in my wallet. Take it and buy yourself something nice," Blake suggested without so much as a blink. "Just put that thing away before someone gets hurt."

"Don't tell me what to do, jerk-off!" The young man nearly screamed, with his voice breaking, and he pushed the steel barrel hard against the scar under Blake's jaw. "Both of you put your shit up, or I'm making fresh cherry pie!"

Blake turned to face him, noticing it was now getting dark outside. He looked past the sight of the pistol to the barely steady hand of the intense robber and noticed that the nine-millimeter's safety switch was on.

"Look, since it's your first time," Blake said steadily. "Just take the money I offered, and get outta here. You don't want this kind of heat, kid."

The young robber's face glistened with sweat, and his upper lip curled back against his teeth. "I told you-"

"You don't have the balls," Blake interrupted, grinning, as he reached up and put his thumb over the young man's trigger finger. "My cash, and you walk. Pull this trigger, and it's gonna be a hard time. You got three seconds."

"Sir, please, just cooperate. You're going to get somebody killed," the clerk pleaded, tying a bag of money closed on the counter.

"One," Blake began, pushing the handgun barrel to his forehead.

The clerk began to panic. He sputtered to find words to reason with either man.

"Get your asqueroso hand off my piece," the robber demanded, with anger and fear mixing on his face.

"Take the money now," Blake repeated. "This is your last chance. Two."

"SAY THREE VATO!" The gunman shouted, challenging Blake. "Somebody bout to be on the FLOOR!"

Blake jammed the young man's finger against the trigger and twisted outward, causing the robber to wince as the gun fell to the floor. Blake reached up with his free hand to the back of the robber's curly hair and clenched a fistful. He brought a knee full force into the angry young man's belly, then pulled hard toward the counter. A solid metallic thud could be heard as the robber's forehead collided with the soft drink on the counter's edge, which sent the young man sprawling to the floor. An impression of the key from the can top was already appearing on the assailant's forehead as the clerk looked over the counter in disbelief.

"What, are you crazy or something?" The bulbous clerk asked, blotting his head and face with a handkerchief.

"Maybe, yeah. What do I owe you?" Blake asked as coolly as when he first asked for the pack of smokes.

"Hey, don't worry about it, friend," The clerk answered with a toothy nervous smile.

"Take the money, friend," Blake sneered. "Or do I have to start counting again?"
The clerk pushed buttons on the register nervously. "Alright, my friend. Five on the pump, so it's uh, twenty-three seventy-one total."

Blake shelled a few bills onto the counter, ignoring the coin change as he walked to his bike to pump gas. He tapped his thumb hard on the top of the can several times to dispense the pressure inside. The released liquid still foamed and overran as he popped the can open and slugged it like a shot. Blake inspected the can with a disappointed look until he found the date stamp as the gas pump stopped at his prepay amount.

"Flat. Expired. Figures," he said to no one as he threw the half-empty drink can across the lot.

He pulled his anaconda helmet on with the visor lifted so he could smoke on the ride, brought the engine roaring to life, and eased back onto the road eastbound.

Only a few minutes away, he found the sign for Shadow Puppets that resembled the matchbook in his pocket. Blake pulled the bike off the road into a parking space in front of a large building with large obstructed windows under the sign. He entered the club with no wait or security. A sign hung on the door that indicated closure for renovation, and the timing of his own club's shutdown made him chuckle.

"Bad week for everybody, I guess," Blake muttered.

When he came onto the main floor, he could see several workers in overalls doing something with the main stage area. Their backs were turned on the floor level, and two others were working on a scaffolding high above the others with some kind of light fixture and pulley riggings. Two technicians were on the floor near the main bar configuring a light sequence on a tablet. Blake tried for a closer look, and one of the techs looked up at him with annoyance.

"You must be Michael," the portly rude worker scoffed. "Alright, boys, that's it for tonight! We'll hit it again in the morning."

Before Blake could correct him, the workers gathered up their tools and made their way out of the building. After a few minutes, Blake made his way to the restroom and muttered under his breath. "Looking forward to another long ride with no answers." He stopped just before coming out of the tucked away hall when he heard voices, sure that one of them belonged to the Michael he knew.

"So I know why you wanted me to come, ma chérie," Michael said. "I thought your boys could get in and out without a fuss, and they drew too much attention. I would have come sooner, but I spent some time with Mr. Fletcher to express my apologies for my mess."

"Aww, so thoughtful," a young woman Blake couldn't see responded quickly. "Mr. Fletcher does like all his little ducks in a row, doesn't he? Everybody has to check with the elusive Atticus Fletcher any time things aren't just as he likes, don't they? You're such a good boy. Did he scratch your ears and give you a snack before he let you come to me?"

High heels clicked across the floor as if timed with a metronome. "Never mind what our sweet Prince Atticus had to say. Soon he'll know better than to impose his demands on me. I'm not his child, and I'm tired of being treated like one. As for you, when you say there will be no problems, I expect you to personally make sure there are no problems. Now because of you, two of my precious children are gone. And what about the girls? You said they were a perfect pair for me. You owed me a protégé, promised me two, and now that puts you four souls in the tank."

Blake recognized the voice and held up his sunglasses to try to see a reflection around the corner of the two who were speaking. With his hair pulled up into a messy ponytail, Michael was talking across the bar counter to a woman that looked just like his last memory of Leila in the subway years ago. His tongue clicked in disbelief, and she looked directly at him in the reflection.

"I TOLD you to come alone," she warned. "How many times will you betray me?"

Blake dropped his glasses when his wrist was grabbed by a large black man with unsettling yellow eyes and baring sharp fangs. Despite resistance, the security guard pulled Blake rather easily toward the bar, where there were now three more men who had a tight hold on Michael from either side and behind. They lifted him onto his back across the bar top while Leila walked toward Blake.

"What the hell are you doing here?!" Michael screamed. "Mon coeur! He followed me, I'm sure of it! I did not invite him here. I would never! After all this time, I would never!"

The pleading only confused Blake more as Leila grabbed him by the throat. She stared into his face taking in every detail.

"Finally updated that hair, big brother." She laughed and met his stare again. Her eyes were turning yellow as she bared long, sharp incisors. "You're still a bit out of style, as usual. Just a little cleaner than I remember. Here for an interview?"

Blake steeled himself with a deep breath, keeping his posture. "What he said is true. I didn't come here with him. I came here to meet someone named Cleo to find out why my place and my girls were attacked. But I guess from what I heard, you're called Cleo now, aren't you?"

"Oh," Leila said with a toothy, heinous grin. "So you lied to your big bouncer here too, did you, Mikey? Well, then he can stay and watch you face justice for your crimes. And after," she turned again and dragged a pointed fingernail under Blake's chin. "We can play a little game with this one." She kept her gaze fixed on Blake but spoke loud enough to address her henchmen. "Drain that thing on my bar, and don't make a mess. Burly Blakey here gets a special front-row seat to the show."

Without hesitation, the three men that held Michael on the bar leaned over him and opened their mouths to bite into his exposed flesh. Michael screamed with an otherworldly terror for mercy. Bleating out more apologies and promises until he fell silent and still.

The large man behind Blake tightened his grip as if he expected a struggle, but Blake held still and watched unblinkingly.

Leila sashayed back to the bar, laughing madly. Her men stopped holding and biting into Michael and stepped back. The men formed a line in front of the bar with crossed arms and satisfied expressions, like dogs who had just been given a special treat.

"Well?" Leila asked. "Did you enjoy that, big brother? Are you here to find out for sure this is what I've become? To try to take me home safe to Mommy and Daddy and that perfect little house in the burbs?"

Blake stared at the body of his boss, lost in his thoughts for a moment as she spoke. Then his eyes rose to Leila's, and he replied, "No."

He tried to step forward but was still held painfully tight at his wrists. "No, I came to see what this place is. I found a matchbook in the pocket of one of the men who attacked my girls. And to ask their boss to set the damages right. But now," he trailed off and looked around the many updated features of this club and then back at Michael. "Now I think I need your help."

"You weren't around much in recent years, Blakey," Leila said as she dragged her fingers across Michael's unmoving body. "But I don't have a lot of history of helping others. Because they usually get lazy and wind up like this one. This very same one who made me what I am years ago, remember? Michael gave me the gifts I needed to achieve anything. And he's about to give me even more." She looked back over to Blake with a pouting mouth. "That doesn't mean you can't do something for me. After all, there is an unsettled debt on the table." She punctuated her answer with a backhand across Michael's lifeless face, which rolled over in Blake's direction.

Blake allowed himself a long blink, his thoughts wrestling in memory and his lip curling in anger. "I guess I don't have much choice, do I?"

Leila grinned widely and held Michael's face over so Blake could see his eyes wide open, frozen in a death state. Those eyes were a blackened abyss that pulled in Blake's gaze.

"No, sweet brother. You don't," she said.

She sank her fangs into Michael's exposed neck as cracked streaks of red and gray filled the void in the corpse's dark eyes like little broken mirrors. Then Michael's eyes became a milky white as the cracked red and gray overtook Leila's wide, deer-like orbs.

Rude Awakening, 1987

Glass from the door's window shattered inward, followed
by a gloved hand reaching for the doorknob. Once the
door swung open, Mickey Gentry came through the frame
headfirst and sprawled on the living room floor with a groan
across the broken glass. Behind him, three men in suits
followed and stepped over him to grab his underarms to drag
him to his feet. Mickey's face was swollen and bloodied from
several hard blows before they entered, and his body hung in
the hands of the men taking him to his leather easy chair in
the corner.

"Dad? Dad!" Blake shouted, running into the room where he
was intercepted by the third strange man.

The suited man pulled the teenage boy to a straight-backed
chair in the undivided kitchen and sat him down. He turned
the chair and pointed Blake toward his beaten father, who
was struggling to breathe and holding his ribs. He stood next
to the young boy, pulled a pistol from under his jacket, then
pushed the barrel into his cheek where he had just begun
growing the fuzz of his first beard hair.

"You said no one would be here," the gunman said. "Nothing
but lies, Mick. Just like always. Where's your old lady?"

Mickey opened his one good eye and gave his son an
apologetic look. "She left," he sputtered. "I told you, she left
this morning. My son, he… he probably just got home from

school."

"It's eight o'clock, Mick," the gunman laughed. "Look at this place, boxes all over, cabinets empty. Looks like you was planning to get outta town. Can't expect me to believe she left all this here and the kid too. Shit, Mickey, it's 1987. Who just ups and leaves their family and house when it's much easier to change the locks and throw out their no-good loser husband and leave your stuff on the lawn?"

"It's… It's cause she," Mickey struggled, adjusting himself in his chair to ease his pain. "She knew you'd find me if I got too far behind."

The gunman relaxed his aim and began waving his gun around the room. "And you did, didn't you? You're always behind. Some role model for your kid."

He walked toward Mickey as Blake sat looking for an advantage to take the gun or run out the door. He picked up a pillow from the couch and shoved it next to Mickey's cheek with the gun barrel pressing against it.

"How you gonna get the money you owe us, Mick? You got nothing. Can't milk the wife anymore with her gone. Nobody left to bail you out. All you got-" he stopped, looking back at the teen, whose face was flushed across his freckles, almost as red as his hair. "This kid is all you got left in the world. What's say we give him the choice, Mickey?"

The gunman walked back over to Blake with his pistol pointed lazily at the floor. "You think you can work off the old man's debt, kid? Come work for us every day, and…"

"No!" Mickey spat as loud as he could muster. "No, he's not any part of this, Louie. I'll get it. I always pay. Always. I'll sell the car and the house. You'll see. I'll pay!"

"These things take time, Mick," Louie assured him. "Time you ain't got." Louie stood beside Blake again and chambered a round in the pistol. Then he placed the gun on the table after removing the magazine. "So kid, you can either walk out of here knowing we are over your shoulder for life after seeing our faces. You could shoot one of us." His thugs began to protest, and he quieted them with a raise of his hand. "Knowing that if you do, the last thing your old man sees is you being beat to death with an empty gun covered in your fingerprints. You could eat the bullet yourself and end your worries. Or-"

Blake took the gun and stood. He didn't hesitate, pulling it up between the intruders to aim at his father. Mickey squeezed his face tight with fear as his son pulled the trigger, though it stubbornly refused to move in his shaking hand. Then, after a moment, he looked back up at the three thugs and his father across the room, confused.

The two suited men burst into laughter as Mickey heaved a sigh of relief. With a cocky stride, Louie closed the gap across the room again.

"Here, let me help you," Louie said, taking the gun from the boy, who was fighting back tears of rage.

Louie turned the pistol sideways in his gloved hands and indicated the safety switch near the trigger loop. Then he turned the gun again to show the boy how to hold it properly with two hands to steady it.

"Let's not have an accident here. Make it deliberate," he said to Blake as he remained stoic.

"Blake," Mickey begged. The fresh smell of urine saturated the air in the room. "Son, I know I done wrong, but we can fix this, you and me."

Blake boldly reached for the gun again and charged across the room with it. He
clicked the safety free and fired the single, chambered bullet point blank into his father's chest. The pistol's slide locked open, but he repeatedly pulled on the pinned trigger.

Louie and his thugs gathered at the door to leave. He turned and addressed the teen boy once more. "Not bad, kid. If you want a job, you got one. If you stay here, you're going to be booked for murder. It don't sound like much of a choice, but it's yours to make."

Objects in the Rearview

Blake left the dressing room, walked out beside the stage, adjusted his collar on a button-down shirt, and carefully began rolling the sleeves past his elbows. The new track lighting installed above the stage was crisp and colorful without being too bright. And those in the rail edge inlay of the stage made the buffed, black wood appear like a wet highway at night. It was glossy and pristine. New poles had been installed, two at the end of the thrust and two more at the edges of a clean, shimmering purple curtain. This would allow for more pairings on stage. It was also intended to increase the cash flow, general entertainment, and comfort of its hopefully returning patrons.

He clicked a few commands into a tablet he purchased earlier that morning, which matched another he'd installed behind the bar, and a third attached to a display arm on the new executive desk in his office. As Blake played with the console screen like a new toy, the lighting changed to grow blinding bright, very dim, or changed through a series of flashing sequences or colors. Also at his fingertips were commands for a new alarm system, and climate control, which he adjusted now to bring the room to a cool sixty-three degrees.

The new floor plan, which included the removal of a wall where the VIP lounge once was closed into a corner room, was now open and lined with a group of three long black leather curling couches with low seating, each separated by thick, sound-dampening partitions. Each of these sections was watched from overhead by a camera and fronted by thin curtains that, in brighter lighting from inside, would show only some shadowed movement to the outside.

Blake set down the tablet on the polished bar top and smoothed his curling hair into a tight ponytail as it was nearly time to bring the public back into the Blush club, formerly known as the Rougir de Vie before its abrupt closing just a few nights ago.

Early for the reopening shift, Brandt came downstairs from the newly furnished loft apartment. He wore the new security uniform, a deep purple blazer, and pressed black slacks. He was burly and broad but not overly tall, with a modern mess of brown hair, over a hedge of eyebrow. He secured the door behind him and looked back over the main floor. "Not sure about the new name, boss," he shrugged. "But we did need something simpler. You sure all the updates were worth the expense?"

"Every penny. The place was falling apart anyway. It's amazing what a few guys on a tight crew can get done in a short time when they work together, isn't it?" Blake grinned as he adjusted the volume setting and cued up some music. "We'll know within a week or two if we're going to do well. I called in a favor to send some business our way." He walked around behind the bar, where another young, fit doorman in a dark purple suit that matched the cooler's updated attire escorted four girls in from the back door to prepare for the start of their shift.

"I'm glad to see the look isn't all that's changed," Brandt noted as he pulled on his lapels and saw that the girls were more showing excitement in the decor as opposed to fear of returning. Then he asked, moving closer with a look over his shoulder, "Did we lose anyone with the shutdown?"

"Well, that is some bad news," Blake started somberly. "Geoff was rushed off in an ambulance after wrecking his car. They told me he didn't even make it to the hospital."

"Geoff is- He's dead?" Brandt's mouth fell open as he looked at the floor.

"It was an accident. He was trying to do the right thing and misjudged a curve," Blake explained. "Also, Cherish told me she's done. But don't worry about her. I want my girls to feel safe here. She said some sleaze she went to school with kept coming in and making her feel uncomfortable even before that mess on Saturday," Blake adjusted the lighting again and put on some house music.

Brandt hung his head. "I'm surprised any of them want to come back in here. Attacked in the VIP lounge, you shooting off that cannon. Even without seeing anything, it crawls inside you. It makes you wonder if something might happen again. If it's gonna be you next time."

"If somebody had been watching the room like they're supposed to, it wouldn't have happened this time," Blake chided. "I understand it's not going to be the same, especially without Geoff. He wasn't just an employee. He was a friend." Blake placed a hand on the bouncer's shoulder. "We still, thankfully, have a business to run, so I need you focused. The damages in the building were minimal. As far as I know, no one called in any complaints, and the remodel was only expensive because I wanted it done in a hurry. And with all that news, we will need to bring in some new faces on the roster. I'll leave that to you if you can handle it. Bring security up to twenty, so you guys can have some nights off, and dancers should be twice as many to leave room for call-offs and part-timers. Plenty for me to do here. On the list of other changes, there's a shipping container on the lot. All the old furniture is out there, as well as dry stock items for the bathrooms and bar. It was easier to gut out some of our closet spaces and expand the main floor. The key is in my top drawer if you need anything from out there."

"You want me to do the auditions? That's a promotional perk I didn't see coming," Brandt looked up and forced a grin. "I won't disappoint you. Uh, hey," Brandt started again with concern as Blake turned away from him to go behind the bar. "Angel and Rose were the ones in the room, right? Have they checked in with you? Rose was the one in the car accident just after, right?"

Blake grabbed a small blue bottle and dabbed on some cologne, "Rose is gonna be fine. She thinks she was thrown from the car on impact before it caught fire. She just needs some time to recover. As long as her sister stays on, I predict she'll be back soon enough."

Brandt gave a sober nod and put on his best customer smile, then made his way to the front door and propped it open for a group of young men taking in the new look of the place with shock and awe. The new cooler took their ID cards and waved over each of them in turn with a magnetized wand as a few of the club's girls came out onto the floor to greet and seat the group.

By the end of the night, the staff were leaving happy. The only altercation from guests had been over a rise in drink prices. Several of the security team mentioned to Blake that cleaning and lockup went more quickly and smoothly than they had in years, despite having to do a few things differently.

Backstage in the spacious dressing room, Tanya collected her tips and balled up the cash to stow into her purse. She pulled its skinny, brown leather strap over her left shoulder and pushed out the back door. She purposely avoided the security escort she'd been told to wait for as part of Blush's new safety policy. Her heels clicked on the concrete outside where the girls went to smoke or cool off between sets where they could hear the thumping music to keep time. She'd been looking in her purse for her keys as she walked when she was blinded by the headlights of a car that had just ground its ignition to start. A shadow could barely be seen through her fingers when she raised a hand to shield her eyes. The shadow figure rose from the car's center and stood there, elbows crooked out with hands on their hips like a disapproving mother.

"Hey loser, don't you know it ain't safe out here for little girls all alone?" the shadow spoke, with the familiar voice of

Tanya's sister. She reached down to flip the lights off and stood back up, laughing. The parking lot lights barely revealed enough to show a wide, lipstick grin on Melissa's pale face.

Tanya dropped her hand and allowed a smile to crawl across her lips. "You better have picked up ice cream," she said with a razor edge in her voice, trying to show anger at Melissa's absence. "We're out."

The drive home flew by while the sisters caught up, often talking over each other and laughing as they tried to ask the same questions about Saturday night. Once back at their apartment, Tanya stripped for a shower. At the same time, Melissa changed into a tiny satin sleepwear set and hugged a pillow between her thighs as she sat on the couch.

Tanya no longer needed the dressing for her neck after drying off, and she let her hair hang down over the scab she could still feel there. She slipped into baggy pajama pants with a drawstring and pulled on a cartoon-patterned spaghetti-strapped top as she walked into the living room. It took a few seconds when her eyes landed on the sight of her sister to blink away the emotion. Once Tanya calmed herself, she let loose a long, quiet breath of relief. Melissa sat very still, with wide, staring eyes fixed right back on hers.

"So, you said it was a long story," Tanya pried again as she had in the car when they started on their way home. "Let me get some spoons, and you can tell me all about it."

A moment later, with one unused spoon sticking out of the far end, Tanya took a large spoonful for herself and placed the carton back on the table between them. With an inquisitive brow raised, she waited impatiently.

"Okay, so I'll tell you what I can remember," Melissa finally said, rolling her eyes. "But you have to promise not to freak out, okay? I'm here, and I'm fine."

Tanya leaned in, taking up her spoon and the carton again. She gave Melissa a half-hearted offer of the ice cream, who waved it off to continue.

"When I woke up, I was just a few feet from a wrecked car. I turned back to see it was our bouncer Geoff in the driver seat, and the car smashed into a brick wall." Melissa continued without allowing Tanya to interrupt with her whimpering mouth full of dessert. "I was dizzy. And I saw blood on my hands. I could even taste blood, so I must have woken up when my face hit the road. Anyway, I was scared and mostly naked, so I just found my way into an alley. On the other side, a car pulled up and offered a ride, so I got inside, and I wound up at Dusty and Kitty's place. I guess they had someone coming to pick them up, and he recognized me or something."

Tanya was still working on another spoonful of melting ice cream with an unrelenting stare as Melissa stopped talking.

"Wait, that's it? So you just got into some dude's car?" Tanya asked, flabbergasted. "What happened to Geoff? What took you so long to call?"

"I didn't do much but sleep," Melissa deflected. "I think.

Either way, I don't remember much else besides being hungry and tired. Anyway, I'm gonna see a doctor in the morning. Early. I made an appointment because I know we can't really afford the emergency room. And I feel fine anyway. Just shook up, you know? I didn't check on Geoff. At the time, if I'm honest, I didn't really know how to. I was pretty messed up." Melissa turned and held the pillow on her lap after crossing her legs in a tight pretzel. "What about you, Tilly? Were you hurt?"

Tanya pressed her hand under her hair, feeling the mostly healed lump of skin, and pulled her hair back down over it. "I was just shaken up. Blake made sure I got home okay," she lied. "Just a bump on the head, nothing to worry about," she said with a dismissing blink and shake of her head.

Melissa eyed the unused spoon in the ice cream carton and reached over and played with it like she might have a bite but then looked up at their front door with a hard gaze. Before Tanya could ask what was wrong, Melissa jumped up from the couch as if her father just caught her with a boy. She had her body tucked and her arms out at her sides like a collegiate wrestler squaring up.

"TILLY, GET OUT OF HERE! NOW, OUT THE BACK WINDOW!"

Tanya sat up, looking around for anything out of place for a long moment, and finally stood just as the front door splintered inward with a thundering ruckus. The figure coming through the door frame was a terrifying shadow of snarling, muscular fur already charging into their apartment at a pace so terrifying Tanya ran down the hall to her sewing room toward the window facing the back lot behind the building. She didn't slow down to grab her purse or phone or look back to see if her sister was following her when she pulled herself outside into the cold night air. The sloped awning below her window did little to brace her fall. She brought most of the aluminum and posts down with her to the ground, where she clambered back to her bare feet to run for their vehicle. She had barely reached the side of their building when their car squealed into view with Melissa at the wheel with the window down and screamed for Tanya to jump in.

Her sister only slowed the vehicle long enough to let Tanya dive in head-first before flooring the gas pedal. Before the tires gained traction, the sound of glass broke out above them, and the beast giving chase landed on top of their car. The impact dented the roof inward and shattered the rear window, but the wolf-like monster slipped off onto the road. Melissa could see the creature in the mirror as she jerked the wheel to turn down a main road away from it and sped up to make a getaway.

Tanya managed to pull herself the rest of the way in and righted herself to sit so she could look back through the shards of glass. She screamed out at Melissa, "What the hell is going on? How did you get past that thing?"

Melissa replied just as loudly, as if trying to match her volume, "I don't know, okay, I just slipped out. We just need to get out of here. Where can we go?"

Tanya looked around the car as if an answer would spell itself out on the dashboard or console. "Um, back to the club? I don't know anywhere else. Then we'll call the police."

Melissa didn't answer, focusing on the road, and drove them back toward their workplace, checking the mirrors every time there was enough streetlight to see behind them. She pointed out that Blake's motorcycle was still parked and pulled their beaten car next to it.

"Before we go in, Tilly, just cool out a sec," Melissa explained. "You need to just ask to use a phone and tell him it was a break-in. I can't believe what I saw, so there's no way he or the police will either. We need a place to stay and can't go home, but I don't want him to just turn us out to some hotel or something."

Tanya nodded frantically, still looking over her shoulder. "That's smart," she agreed, as she tried not to cry again. She threw herself across the seat into Melissa's arms, hugged her tightly, and whispered, "Why is this happening? Why us?"

Melissa hugged her back just as tightly. One of her hands pushed up into Tanya's blonde hair and rubbed until she found the scarred bump underneath. When Tanya pulled away from her, she saw Melissa biting her lip hard and her arms wrapped around herself where Tanya had just been holding her close.

"Missy, you're freezing!" Tanya said quietly as she wiped a sheen of sweat from her neck. "Come on, we can't stay out here barely dressed in the middle of the night."

They found Blake outside near the dumpster tossing a garbage bag and began to tell their story when he interrupted with his hands up. The girls persisted, almost shouting excitedly over each other despite his protest while they spun their version of the home invasion.

"Okay, okay. I get the gist," he cut in. "Come in and get warm. Use the landline behind the bar to call the police. But you know you can't both stay here." At the shock he saw on Tanya's face, he went on, "You're part of an open police investigation, Rose. They came asking questions, and one of the bouncers said you left in his car. But you weren't in the car, and they say they found signs of a struggle, so they're looking for you. Cops asked me where to find you, and I covered. They've been here twice already. So you can't be here now after another incident if you don't want to go downtown for an overnighter." He turned his gaze to Melissa and made his expression as serious as possible through a puff of steaming night air breath. "According to them, witnesses say whoever was with him fled the scene covered in blood as the car caught on fire." Blake put a hand on the back door to the club and leaned as if blocking it from them. He bent his neck toward them and softened his voice. "Do you have somewhere to go?"

"Uh, no!" Tanya butted in, stepping between them. "We came here because there's nowhere else for us to-"

"Yeah. I do," Melissa said flatly. Tanya spun around, her face full of questions. Melissa continued talking to Blake, "If we can just use a phone real quick, a couple of the other girls put me up in their place after the attack. I'll call and convince them to let me lay low there. You have Kitty's number, don't you?"

Tanya's red cheeks dulled slightly, and she blew a cloud of steam in relief. "Oh, right. Then I can go with you, just-"

"No, Tilly," Melissa cut her off again. "Let me go, and I'll find a way to stay in touch. Mr. Gentry is right. I fled the scene after someone died, and I'm afraid if I go to jail, even for a night, Daddy is gonna be up here wondering what became of his good girls with big dreams. Jail, and break-ins, and stripping for money, and all the things he warned us about are just going to bite us in the ass and then we have to go start all over." She took Tanya's hands and looked her in the eyes, her fingers exploring the warm pulsing palms under her cold touch. "You can buy us some time, and I can go be okay there. Maybe the girls can help me find us a new place while we wait on the police and insurance and everything. But before all that," she said, looking over Tanya's shoulder to Blake, "can we get inside out of this cold and get some clothes on? Angel here is shivering while we try to sort all this out."

Tanya hugged her again, openly sobbing this time. She nodded slowly into her sister's shoulder. Tanya didn't wipe away her tears as she turned, taking Melissa's arm to walk into the building. Blake held the door open, taking one more look into the lot before following them inside.

Cruel Intentions

Even though she had called Dusty, when Melissa walked outside, she recognized the car Thaddeus drove waiting in the lot. When the lean, elderly chauffeur stepped out of the driver's seat to open the back door, Tanya's jaw dropped.

Dusty and Kitty peeked out to wave at Tanya. "Hey, don't mind the car. We rented a party limo because we couldn't decide where to go drinking. We were on our way home when you called," Kitty said.

Dusty added as she got out to make room for Melissa to sit in the middle, "We only had one drink, really, but our dates went cold on us and wrecked our plans." She shrugged and smiled. "Better safe than sorry, right?"

Melissa hugged her sister one more time and got into the limousine. "We're gonna get through this. We always do. I'll see you soon."

Once the girls settled inside, Thaddeus gently closed the door and returned to the driver's seat. Melissa sat with her jaw gaping when she saw two men slumped in the opposite bench seat.

"Are they-"

"They're just passed out, doll," Dusty said quickly. "We offered free drinks, and they went overboard real fast.

Competitive young studs trying to impress a couple of girls out on the town. It's a good thing we don't get sick anymore because they sure did."

"But why are they here?" Melissa asked in a hushed tone like someone might hear them.

Kitty shrugged, twirling a tendril of hair. "You were on the way. We're dropping them off at the bar where we found them up the street."

When the car came to a stop again, Dusty waved at a group of young men hanging out in the parking lot. "Hey guys, remember us? Your friends couldn't hold their beer. Can you give us a hand?"

They approached as a group of three, and one, without wasting any time, said, "We can give you girls more than a hand. Three of you, three of us. Too bad for Bobby and Rick, huh?"

Dusty smiled back at the other girls and opened the door, pulling a tiny handgun from her purse and holding it to her chin like a thinker's finger. "I think maybe you Lotharios can get your little buddies out of my car without a fuss. Or I can play target practice on all the parts of a man I don't need to have a good time. Your call, honey."

The three guys began gibbering apologies as they hustled to get in and drag their unconscious friends out of the car. "Oh, Christ! They puked on each other." Another turned his head, trying to hold onto a limp body as he dragged him backward, "It's all over me now, asshole! Thanks a lot!" The last, climbing out of the car and pushing out from behind, shouted, "Alright, shut up. I ain't trying to get shot. Just grab him, and let's get outta here!"

Dusty closed the door when she returned, laughing as soon as her window was up. "Well, not what I had planned, but more fun than I expected."

Kitty chimed in, "It is still a party night. We were just trying to pre-game a little. You picked a good night to come home, sweetie. We just need to pick up our guest of honor, and we'll be on our way."

The car came to a stop again near the downtown theater, and Thaddeus opened the car door so the girls could see a man laying on a bus bench with his thin beige coat wrapped tightly around himself. He was maybe twice the age and half the size of the college boys they had with them earlier. He had an overgrown black beard peppered with gray that nearly hid the long lines on his face.

Dusty leaned out toward him. "Hey, handsome, when's the last time you had a bite? We want you to come with us, out of this cold, and get you a hot meal. Whaddya say?"

The man sat up and nodded dumbly. Then, he walked over to the car with a look of concern at the driver as if some catch was about to snag.

"Come on, sugar, shake a leg," Dusty added with her hand extended for the man to help himself climb inside.

On the short drive, Dusty and Kitty prodded the man with questions and guesses about who he was and how he wound up living on the streets. He had barely begun to mutter responses as they cut him off again and again with more questions and lay on thick compliments about what his life must have been like up until now.

The more they spoke, the more Melissa's head turned between them, like watching a close tennis match at Arthur Ashe, her eyes growing wide and her mouth gaping. When the car stopped in front of the Valiant Manor, she was quick to get out of the car and out of the middle of the other two.

Thaddeus escorted Melissa to the door himself, separating her from the other two who took the vagrant man toward the kitchen. "Come, miss. We must get you properly dressed for supper. I've taken the liberty of selecting an appropriate dancing ensemble for when you meet Master Fletcher tonight."

"But I thought you said I shouldn't meet him before I-"

"Preparations are in place for the evening. You will have ample opportunity to tame your thirst before proper introductions are made." Thaddeus had a soothing, fatherly tone and said nothing more as he took her to her room to clean up and change.

Inside the room, she saw at first a deep, lengthy white box on the chest at the foot of the bed. It was wrapped with a silky black ribbon and had a small note attached that read, -Welcome Home, -Atticus-.

She pulled slowly at the ribbon, stretching the moment a bit longer. She looked over her shoulder at the closed door as if someone was standing there watching the way a parent watches their child on Christmas morning. Melissa lifted the lid and unfolded the tissue paper to reveal a shimmering formal-length gown. It began at the top with sequined, peacock-inspired embroidery over a tightly woven charcoal mesh. The single sleeve of the one-shoulder dress ended in a finger loop and twinkled in feathery green and black. She had to stand to lift the entire dress to see it in full. The gown had an indigo skirt featuring a hand-stitched folded peacock tail down from the hip across billowy satin. Its back was formal-length, with a knee-high front, and its visible underlay mirrored the mesh top.

The dress fit almost as if her sister had hand-made it to Melissa's measurements. Melissa took a few steps around barefoot before going to the closet to choose a pair of strappy black court dancing shoes with mid-high heels detailed with rhinestones. She returned to the chest and moved the box to sit down. When she felt the gift package still had some weight to it, she looked in and saw a dark mask. It was shaped to cover all but the left eye and cheek. The mask had a broad arrangement of fanned feathers on the opposite side to compliment the peacock design on the gown. The matte charcoal face was sparingly sprinkled with silvery glitter.

She heard a tap on the door and the familiar voice of Thaddeus. "Miss, may we expect you to join us soon?"

Melissa went to open the door to find the servant standing profile in a white tailcoat tuxedo, with a mask covering the upper half of his face. His mask was skull-like, with bony fingers that spread across his jaws and mustache. Above the nose bridge clung an emerald scarab.

"Look at you!" she said too loudly. "Now I won't feel so overdressed. What do you think?" Melissa struck a pose and twirled around, looking over her shoulder at how the skirt moved.

Thaddeus offered a smile she could see met his eyes even with the elaborate mask. "Stunning, miss. May I escort you down to the ballroom?"

"Hold on," Melissa said with her hands going up into her hair, beginning to twist one side into a braid. "I need to get my hair up real quick and put on this gorgeous mask. Tanya showed me a trick for a quick updo I think will be perfect. What's with your getup? You look amazing!"

She wrestled her curls of hair into a loose braid on either side and tailed them together. With the meeting tail of hair, she wrapped it all into a bun with rebellious wisps and asked Thaddeus to tie on her mask. Melissa shot a look at the mirror that only reflected Thaddeus standing and fiddling with his hands behind where she should have been standing.

"I am not one to be left out when it comes time for celebration, my dear," Thaddeus said. "All of the time spent preparing for such things is not to be wasted just because I serve the manor."

"I wish I could see what this all looks like together. I just don't get it."

"All will come to you in time, child," Thaddeus said as he finished securing the mask cords. "But we really must go now." He held out his arm for her to take and walked them down the hallway to the top of the staircase.

When they reached the beginning of the banister, Melissa looked down over the main hall, where a dozen or so people waited quietly, looking up through masks of their own at Melissa and Thaddeus. There was a demon mask in black and red, a lacy eye mask in bright blue, a sinister jester mask, a green faerie mask, and more, each worn with mostly complimentary formal outfits fit for a proper masquerade.

Only one among them wore no mask. The vagrant man the girls had picked up from the theater stood out from the middle of the crowd, freshly shaved in a rather plain, black tuxedo. He appeared to be both delighted and confused, and quite possibly on the brink of tears. Thaddeus took the first step down, which cued Melissa to come along, and he presented her to the party below as if she were the featured guest at a debutante ball.

"The most recent addition of our proud and illustrious family here at Valiant," Thaddeus began, demanding their already rapt attention. "I have been given the esteemed privilege to introduce to you Miss Melissa Renee Johnston, an unparalleled beauty whose vibrant youth may never betray her in the years yet to come. Join me in welcoming Miss Johnston with our timeless tradition of the first dance, which we, of course, offer to our honored guest, Mr. Douglas Grady."

The maskless vagrant looked up again at the calling of his name and smiled as proudly as he could. He offered his hand to her as Thaddeus moved aside to usher in a quartet of string players, who had also dressed accordingly for the occasion, to sit on one side of the room where they began to play. The music was a classical piece. Mr. Grady took his first step into the tune, wrapping his free hand around Melissa's waist and nervously squeezing her hand in his other. She followed his lead in a simple, elegant box step with no embellishment. The other party guests gently applauded as the dancers made their first movements together, then began to make pairs and danced in a sort of fluid circle around the first two.

Over Mr. Grady's shoulder, Melissa noticed only one figure, of masculine stature, watching alone. His full knightly mask of gold remained fixed on her. She looked back to her partner, his face of joyful disbelief began to show signs of confidence. He offered length to his reach, leading her into a slow spin, and brought her close when she finished, looking around to appraise the crowd for approval. When there was no protest, he ventured again, putting Melissa and himself side by side, adding twisting steps. Her skirt fanned and twirled slightly as she matched his movements again. This time when he pulled her close again, he laughed out loud, and Melissa's gaze locked onto his exposed throat.

The circle of dancers moved closer, closing the distance as if encouraging a more intimate coupling. The first song had ended, and in the time between starting the next one, the gold knight had moved through the crowd and took his place behind her. He began to untie Melissa's mask and pulled it away from her face before she could protest.

Douglas looked into her eyes and said, "I hope you'll just call me Doug. This is all just too much to-"

She leaned forward as he spoke and pressed her lips to his neck. She bared her teeth and pierced the flesh where it pulsed and gushed past her tongue with a warm, smooth stream. A long moment passed before she felt a strong grip pull her away from Doug, who gasped and reeled into a new partner. Mr. Grady's face was a mix of fear and euphoria, but he made no attempts to protest. The woman who took him looked directly at Melissa and suckled sweetly from the same place on his neck. Another woman cut in a moment later, wasting no time on ceremony, and bit Douglas swiftly as he moaned aloud, his eyes wide with mixed emotions. This woman with her gypsy veil mask of coins let him go to another who tore off and flung away a kabuki-style disguise but took her time to find Melissa's face with her wide eyes. She licked a long trace of the contour of his throat before slowly bending in for a drink. Melissa recognized Dusty's face with a teasing expression before the vagrant was spun off to another woman to have a turn. The men closed in as well then, taking either of their honored guest's wrists and latching on until the entire party had swarmed him, where Melissa could no longer see.

In the arms of the gold-masked man, Melissa followed into a waltz with the quartet's tempo. She stole glances over his broad shoulder, licking her teeth and lips until her attention crept tightly into the chest of the mystery man and his hypnotic dance.

Tanya sat in the refinished dressing room with a pen and notepad, drawing ideas for dresses she might use for the stage. Several balls of wadded paper were scattered across her vanity. She scribbled across another page before tearing it out to crumble in her hands. She recrossed her legs with a huff and looked up at the clock while her foot bobbed restlessly.

She stood barefoot with her hands on her hips, still wearing the pajamas she had arrived in the night before, plus an oversized hooded sweatshirt Blake offered her. She had already painted her finger and toenails, paced the stage, played with the lights, and walked a few laps around the club in the few hours since Mr. Gentry retired to the loft just before sunrise. Tanya returned to the dressing area again, opened the box of untouched pizza with a grimace, and closed it again. She went back to the clothing rack, pulling a few out that had frayed hems or broken straps.

Tanya looked at the clock again, dropping her shoulders forward, then flipped open a small pencil box on her vanity that had a few colors of thread and a few needles stuck in a tiny grotesque jeweled mink pincushion. She chose to fix the shoulder strap of a slinky red nightie, seeing that she had the most thread in a matching color.

After a dozen or so attempts at threading her needle, she slammed her fists down on the tabletop. Tanya barely recognized herself in the mirror. Strands of wild hair hung around her face, which was haggard and puffy. Her bottom teeth pushed out, and she glared at her reflection as if challenging it to say something cross. She inhaled deeply, fending off tears, and made a disgusted face from the smell. Tanya pulled the sweater up over her nose and inhaled again before peeling it off and tossing the garment into a corner of the floor.

She grabbed a couple of items from the costume rack and took them to the main room. After a glance toward Blake's loft, she shook her head and instead went toward the champagne room for the only other shower access in the building. On her way, she noticed Blake's office door was left slightly open and went closer to take a look inside.

"You can't sleep either, huh?" she asked hopefully, pushing the door open only to find no one there to hear her.

A motion sensor turned on bright lights overhead when she stepped through the door. The office, though empty, was half-lit from the screens of security camera feeds around the club. Tanya held her change of clothes closer in her arms and walked around the room, seeing the updated decor of this room for the first time. Some pictures were on display in a wooden cabinet with a glass front. Mr. Gentry was in many of the photos, with his arm around or in some way presenting one of the girls who danced there at the club. Some were celebrity guests who visited once, and some were specially featured talent who had made their fame from the adult film industry.

Tanya placed her clothes on the edge of the desk, which had very little on it. A propped daily comic calendar stood close to a tablet that controlled many of the new electronic features within Blush, and the keys to Mr. Gentry's motorcycle lay on the corner of the desktop.

She couldn't help but scoff at her findings as she sat in the large leather chair behind the clean desk. She let the chair rotate smoothly to one side and then pushed it the other way. "Why even have this great big desk if you aren't using it for anything? What a waste."

She reached for Blake's office tablet and found it had no password lock. Sliders appeared on the screen for lighting, with several application widgets in a row across the bottom labeled for lights, sound, and video. Tanya selected the video with a fingertip and chose the camera feed for the office, where she saw the room in real-time from a corner camera point of view. She flicked her finger again to the rewind feature and watched herself enter the office in reverse, and then it grew dim as the motion sensor in the feed had not yet been activated. Rewinding further, the screen blurred and flipped like an old floor model television relying on the poor signal of a rabbit ear antennae to attune to a station. With not much left of the recording, she continued to slide the timer bar on the screen backward until the picture was clear again.

She pressed play to see Blake sitting at the desk when the door opened. He had been sitting with a mess of papers on the desk, looking through them. Then he hurried to gather them into a thick, beaten file folder and hastily tossed the mess into a bottom drawer as an unfamiliar figure entered the room. The feed had no sound, went hazy, and again resembled a scrambled signal. Tanya scrolled the timer bar to see this went on for over an hour before returning to where she entered the office and activated the motion sensor.

Tanya backtracked her actions on the tablet and returned the device to the desk, eyeing the keys near it. She lowered her gaze to the bottom drawer, where a piece of paper was wedged into the lip of the drawer, and looked back up at the closed office door. She took the keys from the desk and found the smallest one on the ring to try the drawer and turned it to find it had been left unlocked.

She pulled it open, and the wedged paper fell in over an open, loose file. She flicked her fingers across the documents in the folder while slinking down to the floor on her knees. The contents were like a scrapbook that had yet to be organized. Tanya hunched over the open drawer and carefully leafed through the thick pile of papers. Mostly it was clippings from newspapers, but it also had a few from magazines, scribbled notes, pieces of maps, some brochures, and some sticky pad notes throughout with phone numbers and addresses. News stories of odd happenings in the local area were the bulk of the clippings. There were several pages of missing person cases, a few articles on car accidents, one was a report of a derailed train, and some about local building fires.

The motion sensor lights clicked off, and Tanya was startled enough to bang her head against the desk. She slammed the drawer closed, ripped the key out, and tossed them on the desk. Tanya gathered up her clothes and hurried out of the office to the champagne room to finally go for a shower.

Simon stopped by to check up on Tanya in the early morning, but her car was nowhere in sight. He was about to turn the wheel to leave when he noticed the door to her upstairs apartment was open. He turned the key off and left it, then crossed the road to ascend, finding the door was destroyed. He reached into his coat breast for his pistol, thinking better than to pull it in exposed daylight, and stepped in through the broken door frame.

"So much for my new door," he muttered.

Inside, the door lay in pieces, the coffee table was overturned, and he could see claw marks in the archway to the living room. Simon took his time slowly looking around, finding two purses and cell phones, a spilled carton of ice cream, and a window broken in one of the bedrooms. No glass shards inside the room told him whoever did this was thrown out, or jumped out in a hurry. The bed under the window had been pushed away from the wall slightly, and the linens on the mattress were strewn and torn, also from animalistic claws much like his own when the moon got the better of him. He took a second look at the marks on the archway and noted a middle stroke was missing, leaving only three marks when he expected four.

Simon gathered up the purses and phones and turned toward the front door, but stopped when he heard voices outside. An older man was responding to questions from what sounded like a very collected younger woman. He peeked out the damaged window again to see a police cruiser parked in front of the building and went back inside to look for a better exit. He soon found the open window where the twisted remains of an awning had collapsed below. He judged the leap, slightly elongated his features, bristling with heavy fur, and jumped with canine flexibility to miss the damaged metal pieces. He landed quietly, shaping back to his former self with a quick look to be sure no one saw. Simon then quickly made his way to the back alley before walking to the main street with the purses tucked inside his coat. He crossed the street, climbed back into his jeep, and slowly drove away. Once the police vehicle was no longer in his mirrors, he turned west, away from the girls' apartment.

He drove on but let off the accelerator when the wind changed direction. It drew his nose to something in the back seat of his jeep, and he turned again to go over the bridge away from the city. A few minutes later, he was on a familiar dirt road leading into the woods toward his hunting grounds. Simon parked the jeep in the lane leading to his cabin. He stepped out, brandishing a heavy unpolished handgun from the holster under his arm.

"How long have you been tailing me, Reno?" Simon asked as he slowly moved around to the back of the vehicle and waited a moment, then let loose a feral growl.

"Alright, alright. You got me," a voice came from the mess of rumpled blankets and rucksack in the back seat. A broad, tall man with leathery, tanned skin emerged from the blanket with raised hands. His crew cut was parted by a long pale scar, and he wore a crooked grin. "Senses are sharper than I thought.

But a gun? You gettin' lazy or what?"

"It ain't for show if that's what you're asking," Simon retorted. "What do you want?"

"Hey, listen, you wouldn't have taken any more kindly to a house call. It's been a while, and I was surprised to see you, that's all." Reno fully exited the jeep and stood in front of Simon in the middle of the dirt lane. "Can I put my hands down? I just want to talk."

"No games. Tell me what you were doing in the apartment." Simon showed no frustration on his face, but his tone was accusing.

Reno took a step back and leaned against the parked vehicle. "Okay, that's fair. I'll go first. Then it's your turn to tell me what are you doing with a sucker girlfriend."

After a moment with no reaction from Simon, Reno impatiently stood again and started pacing the length of the bumper, with the sun peeking through the trees from high above. "That was my business there. Those girls and the whole club they work with are all suckers. But these two are living in the suburbs like normies, man."

"We've been over this," Simon answered. "Vampires are not the pack's problem. I thought by now you'd be over this or learn from the mistake that put you on the outside."

Reno's grin disappeared. He was seething. "The pack is still blind, man. Obviously, you are too. You were in that apartment with them. What? Are you their chauffeur? Their bodyguard? Are they paying you to watch the door in the daytime? Or," he stopped pacing and glared at Simon. "Maybe you're sleeping with them? Some kind of blood doll or something?"

Simon said nothing for a moment, but as the accusations flew, his lip curled into disdain. "I don't appreciate your nose in my business. You were told to move on, and you haven't even turned a page yet. How many years have you wasted obsessing over this?"

"SUCKERS MURDERED MY WIFE! You know what it's like to carry something like that, don't ya pal?" Reno's grin returned, but not like the cocky expression before. He was crazed and hunched forward, pushing clouds of steaming breath through clenched teeth.

"Yeah, so what? Everybody's got baggage," Simon replied. "The pack put you out because you were a loose cannon bent on revenge. You were reckless. You retaliated and killed with no proof-"

"SO WHAT?! NO PROOF??" Reno spat. He lunged forward with rage as his features grew to monstrous proportions.

Simon fanned the hammer of his revolver, firing two shots before the beast within took over his human form, which grew in proportion to meet the werewolf before him.

BOUGHT WITH BLOOD

Birds perched high in the trees above them flew off, cawing in warning, as the visceral growls below echoed through the leafless forest.

True Lies

The sky swirled with storm clouds that shrouded the stars and half-moon. Fingers of leafless branches stretched out, unable to grasp each other as they swayed and whispered until the voice of the wind became a wicked, high-pitched howl.

A stinging drop of rain landed in Simon's eye, and he blinked hard several times. He slowly lifted his arms with stiffness and difficulty until he could reach his face to knead his brow and jaw. He carefully rolled his neck to one side and then the other, with nothing but frolicking dead leaves racing by until he locked his gaze on a dark, thick lump a few yards away. He noticed a trail of blood toward the body and dragged his fingers across the hard ground to touch a prominent spot of puddled blood. Simon brought it to his nose and rubbed his fingers together. He watched the body closely and slowly stood, stretching his limbs and bending at the waist while he suppressed groans with a wince.

He stepped closer, noting the gory remains of an adult black bear and its twisted limbs as it lay dead. Simon drew his fingers across his chest, slowly tracing new scars that matched the size of this animal's claws. With another look around as the rain poured over them, he bowed his head and placed his hand over the broad back of the broken creature. Simon inhaled the stirring earthly bouquet blending around himself and finally stood with his soiled face toward the sky. He searched the landscape for anything familiar and blew a gout of steam to watch the wind take it before he began to plod away from his kill.

Tanya woke with a stir and quickly sat up from her vanity as she heard heavy approaching footsteps. Brandt was pulling on his sport coat over a sleeveless, black t-shirt and cocked his head at her disapprovingly.

"I thought we were clear about the new security guidelines, Angel," he chided. "You're supposed to be escorted in with a boun- I mean, doorman so we can be sure you're safe. What are you doing here early anyway?"

She pushed a fake smile across her lips and stretched her arms high above her head. "Mr. Gentry invited me to stay last night after my car got slammed. I just came down here to fix one of my dresses before we open."

Brandt pushed his lips together and nodded. "You alright? I saw it in the lot, and it looks like hell."

She dragged out her words slowly to form an answer as she spoke. "The car was hit when it was parked. I wasn't in it. Now I just need to make some extra tonight for a tow."

He shook his head and shrugged, "Speaking of extra, Mr. Gentry says he's looking to add some talent to the club. So I'm hoping you'll help the new girls feel right at home here."

"Uh, sure," she agreed quickly. "Rose and I are real good at making friends." She looked over her shoulder where Melissa should have been sitting next to her for a few seconds. "I'll make sure to tell her when she gets here."

Brandt put a hand out with a "Come here," gesture. "Oh hey, since nobody else is here yet, toss me your keys so I can move the car around back. All that busted glass is not a good look for the customers."

She nodded back and scooped up her car keys to throw them. When he left, she waited a minute to be sure he was far away before standing to look after him. She grabbed a pair of black sling-backs and carried them on two fingers toward Blake's office. The dull purple lights were already on in the main stage area, which made it easy to avoid kicking into chair legs as she walked briskly to the door.

When she saw the bright light on, she knocked and pushed the door open. "Hey, Brandt says we're gonna be hiring a bunch of new girls. Does that mean some of us need to look for new work?"

"No, nothing like that," Blake answered. He spun his chair around to greet her. "We put some glow on this place, but that can't undo what was seen here. And even though you came back, I'm sure you don't really want to be here. So I'm hoping you might do some scouting for us. I put Brandt in charge of the actual hiring, but he doesn't have the time to go out and advertise for us."

"Wait, and I do? Missy and I are in the mid-"

"Hold on," Blake said, putting his hands up. "I considered

you don't have a place or a car right now. And I was thinking about how I could help with that. I called ahead to get your car towed in the morning. You can sort out insurance and all that once the adjusters get in touch." He stood and pulled a credit card from his pocket. "This card has an advance on it for recruiting, lodging, taxi service, food, or whatever other expenses."

"Why are you offering all this?" Tanya asked wide-eyed as she leaned on his desk and dropped her shoes when she crossed her arms. "This doesn't sound anything like you."

Blake reached down to pull a drawer open and leafed through it to find a stapled pack of papers. "Most girls don't come here with a three-page resumé. Most girls haven't lost their asses in the space of a week. And most of the girls think I don't know how to manage a business. I never expected you'd set foot in here again after what happened, but you've shown real moxy. Not to mention you have a degree." He pointed at the space on the page, noting her education.

Tanya shook her head in disbelief. "Well, I mean, it's not a degree yet. And it's for fashion design, and I have a semester left of-"

"And a minor in entrepreneurship. I can read. Close enough for me," he cut her off again. "You fix outfits, even design your own. You and your sister create your stage routines and set lists. You have a mind for moving up and running your own business. But there is really nowhere to go with that working here. And I think I know just the place for you to get a good look at some new prospects for our business and maybe a chance to move on to something better suited for yourself." Blake turned the papers on his desk toward her and sat back down. "Take this with you," he said, adding a business card to the top that read -Shadow Puppets-. "The woman who runs the place used to work for me. She moved on to build herself a nice stake. I think you should meet her and see if she has something for you."

"I don't know what to say." Tanya reached down to pick up her shoes and slipped them on instead. "Does this mean once I do all this, I'm fired?"

He half-grinned and leaned forward. "You're not interested? If it sounds like a bad deal, I'm sure I could take a chance and put this card in someone else's hands. I thought you were my best choice. But if you'd rather stay here and pluck singles out of your G-string, I'm happy to keep you on the payroll."

Tanya stared at him hard for a long moment and looked down at the papers and credit card, then toward the drawer in which he kept the thick file. Her brow furled, and she took a deep breath. "How… How did you do your hiring before? I mean, don't you and Mr. Laurent just audition anyone who comes asking?"

"Michael and I have severed ties," Blake said flatly. "The, uh, incident was an eye-opener for both of us, and he didn't want to rebuild, so I bought him out." He stood again and addressed her directly. "So rather than a strip club that preys on young women who have no other options, I'd like to try having someone with your experience approach new hopefuls who actually know how to dance and want to make some good money doing it at a refurbished gentleman's club."

"So, how much is on the card?"

"I pre-loaded this with twenty-five hundred," he answered. "Which reminds me, if you need more to cover medical for you or your sister, I'm happy to cover it. With the shift in paperwork, it might take some time to drum up a compensation case, so just let me know what you need and keep receipts."

"A hotel, some appropriate clothes for an interview. Maybe a checkup." She plucked the credit card out of his hand and bit her lip. "Time off from the floor to do some recruiting. For me and Missy."

He nodded and rechecked the time. He tapped a few spots on the tablet, and music began thumping in the stage room. "Your set starts in a few minutes. Do you need anything else from me before you start your last night on stage?"

"Think you can cue up a tall iced coffee for me? Caramel and whipped cream?" She asked with a syrupy sweet tone and a broad smile.

He grinned back and bowed his head as if he'd just lost an argument. "Demoted just that fast from club owner to gopher. I'll see if someone delivers. I'm hoping for a full house tonight. Now get out of here before the girls think I'm playing favorites."

***

Melissa took the arm of a husky bouncer on the way into Blush through the rear entrance. Once inside, she looked down the row of new mirrors on the vanity wall and made a face before she turned away from them to hang up her jacket. She looked for the listed set rotation, which was now displayed on a monitor that hung just below a bright red digital clock.

When Tanya came around the corner to the backstage area, she squealed with joy and hugged her sister tightly. "I have some good news- Oh god, your hair needs some help!" She spun Melissa toward the closet rack and began to pull at the mess of hair until she managed to make low pigtails. "Pick something to wear. You're on right after me. They split us up tonight, but that will just help me keep my dirty little secret."

Melissa slipped into the routine of rushing her change and reached back to unzip her skirt before stepping into another stretchy, pink one that covered much less. She turned to face Tanya, who was already pulling off her sweatshirt so Melissa could squirm into a tight, sheer camisole.

"I gotta go," Tanya whispered, grabbing Melissa's hands with a squeeze before she scampered away in heeled boots to the stage.

Melissa eyed the setlist again, noting she didn't have even one shared moment on stage with her sister but instead had been paired with just about everyone else in a rotation. Kitty approached her closely when she was alone and handed Melissa a neon garter belt to cinch on her upper thigh.

"If you're tempted to have a few sips tonight, make sure you lick over the wound," Kitty said just above a whisper. "We don't want any messes. And early is better than later. Drunks can get you drunk, druggies can get you high, and it takes a long time to come down." She left Melissa's side quickly with a playful swat across her backside, then strutted away toward the exit to the main floor.

It was a very busy shift that played host to a series of hot seat dances for two bachelor parties, and one customer requested a private dance to celebrate his recent divorce. The scruffy divorcee claimed Melissa looked just like an ex-girlfriend from college, and he tipped her with a stack of bills when she finished a languid, slow lap dance.

With all the paid requests, there were longer breaks than usual between sets for many of the girls. Though some dancers that were favored seemed to be on the floor almost all night with few chances to change outfits or touch up their look. Melissa was offered extra money nearly every time she came off stage and spent quite a lot of the night selling table dances to patrons who wanted to be chatty and keep her attention.

When it was time to shut down for the night, Melissa quickly changed into her street clothes and went to sit on one of the bench seats near the Champagne Room. When Tanya came out to find her, Melissa was still organizing her cash to fit into the inside pocket of her jacket.

"Time just dragged on tonight," Tanya complained. "I need to show you something."

Tanya pulled a white credit card out of her boot and flashed it once before putting it back out of sight into the front pocket of Blake's oversized hoodie. She sat in the booth bench seat snugged up tight against Melissa.

"You got tipped with a gift card?" Melissa joked dryly. "Thought you were better than to take a scam, T."

"Noooo, it's not some random used gift card. Fool me once," Tanya added to the joke with an exaggerated roll of her eyes. "It was from Blake. He's fronting the cost of a hotel for us and gave me a lead on another job. Something that isn't getting naked for obnoxious drunk guys."

Melissa shrugged. "Where's the fun in that? I like this job."

"I mean, yeah, the money is alright. But we got hurt here unless you forgot already." Tanya's tone sobered. "We need to think farther than tomorrow."

"And all that sounds great. But you're also the one always telling me not to count my chickens before-"

"Daddy says that," Tanya broke in.

"Whatever. Daddy is probably right," Melissa shot back. "Anyway, I'm just saying we shouldn't burn this boat while we're still floating on it."

"Missy, this could be everything we ever wanted. We could go home this Christmas as career women and not have to lie about what we do!" Tanya's face scrunched up as she looked at Melissa. "We won't have to be apart ever again. This week has been a nightmare thinking I lost you, and then today you never called, and-"

"And you don't think I've had it rough?" Melissa stood up and took a few steps before leaning in close over her sister. "You said we'd be fine. You said we were ready to leave home. You said you'd take care of me, and you just can't keep any of your damn promises. Fashion was your dream. College was your plan, and none of that shit is working for me, okay? Could you have gotten Dusty's number from Blake at any time today?"

"Missy, I-"

"Don't!" Melissa pointed a stiff finger in Tanya's face. "Stop putting pressure on me to do what you want, and maybe think for a moment that we don't need to be sewn together at the hip! I wanted to party. And to be young. And to have boyfriends, maybe girlfriends. And to stay out all night and sleep all day. And not be such a fucking adult all the time! I made almost four hundred tonight without even sweating off my foundation, and you want me to up and leave?"

Tanya had already begun to cry blackened streaks of mascara down her angry, betrayed expression. "Fine. If that's what you want, fine. I'm not your keeper. Do what you want." Tanya also stood and took a few steps to make Melissa back up. "The difference between you and me, the REAL difference, is that you have always been allowed to say no to me. And not ONCE have you given me the same damned courtesy. I've been taking care of us. I have made all the sacrifices while you do whatever you want. I am YOUR little sister, and I should never have had to parent you just because YOU won't ever grow up and take care of YOURSELF!"

Melissa turned to find that most of the girls were still in the stage room, watching the argument intently. Some looked away or made themselves busy. When she turned back around, Tanya was already walking away toward the front door, where Brandt was waiting to escort her out.

Melissa turned to Dusty and pulled out her pigtails. "Am I still good to get a ride?"

Dusty nodded quickly, "Sure, honey. Let's get you home."

Melissa stopped at those words and took a moment as if waiting for something. She looked back to see Tanya had already vanished from sight, just like her own reflection. She stepped into Dusty's embrace to walk out the back together. Kitty joined her on her other side and put an arm around her as well.

Gotta Break a Few Eggs

Tanya made a tidy two-egg omelet in a saucepan that had to be washed of dust and clinging grease before use. She had already paced around the nearly 700 square feet of space where clutter didn't obstruct her way in the fourth-floor efficiency apartment near the university. She was greeted through the above sink window by a neighbor on his balcony across the alley. He had stepped out to light a cigarette wearing a fluffy pink robe that was much too small, and his receding orange hair stood out to one side. Though he seemed friendly enough, she broke eye contact quickly when he smiled with a missing front tooth and tucked a hand inside the robe to scratch himself.

She banged a spatula against the edge of the pan loudly until she saw the broad-backed cooler rouse from sleep on his Murphy bed in the main room.

"Hey, it's too early for all that noise. I thought all you girls slept all day between shifts," Brandt asked as he threw his legs over the side to sit up.

"Well, some of us do more than just take our clothes off for money. Like, go to school, have day jobs, and keep up some sense of normalcy by eating breakfast at breakfast time." Tanya offered him the paper plate of eggs with a set of disposable utensils and a paper towel.

"A guy could get used to this kind of treatment-"

"As he should," she cut him off. "When you finally find that very special someone who actually wants to give it." Tanya stepped around the bed and sat on the opposite corner from him. "But really, I just needed to get you awake enough to drive me back. Or at least to call me a cab. I still don't have my phone back, so I'm kinda stuck without your help."

"So last night," Brandt spoke between bites. "You just used me for a ride, huh?"

"Listen, I'm sorry if you thought more was going to happen. I don't remember saying anything that would have led you on, but I just needed to get out of there, and you saw my car."

"No, you're right. I guess I just thought maybe…forget about it." He finished his omelet and went to the kitchen to discard his disposable wares.

She looked across the bed and followed him with her eyes as he walked away in just boxer briefs. He wasn't just fit, but lithe, more like a gymnast build than a typical footballer or heavy lifter, like most guys she had met in college or her customers.

"So, how did you wind up working for Mr. Gentry? Are you just in it to meet girls?"

"Well, as you can see, that's going great, isn't it?" He turned back into the main room and started to dress himself. "I guess it's kind of like anything else. I had no job experience, and I'm over six feet tall. So I could have done a labor job and grind away. I applied to learn how to bartend but was no good at it. Mike said I looked like I could kick some ass, so he fit me to be a bouncer. The money is too good to go do anything harder, and now I got a promotion, a cleaner look, and the drive ain't too far."

"You look like you could have had a scholarship for something bigger than handling some unruly idiots in a nightclub," she suggested. "Were you a high school athlete? Baseball or something."

Brandt gave her a long look with a grin. "Uh, no. But as long as you don't say anything. I was a geeky, lanky kid who was clumsy in every possible way. I couldn't ball, I couldn't run, I was picked on a lot, and had test anxiety like you wouldn't believe. So in school, I was a whole lotta nothing." He buckled his belt and pulled on a long-sleeved grey shirt.

Tanya slipped on her shoes when he grabbed his keys to walk out. "So, what? You got a gym membership and turned it around?"

"Well, not exactly. I also was a foster kid, and that came with a lot of bullshit you don't even want to know. I barely got a diploma and couldn't leave home any faster. I came here where I found out my only living relative was an aunt, who barely had room for me to sleep on a couch." He walked Tanya to his car and held the door for her. "She was a good cook, and I was putting on pounds fast, and I had no job. She taught yoga and worked nights at a dance studio. She got me a job sweeping up, and I took some classes and got fit. But then she got sick real bad. Docs said the problem was bigger than a flu or whatever, and the next thing we knew, she was on chemo treatments. I lost my job from taking all that time off to be with her and got stuck with all her bills too."

"That's a lot to pack into a short time," Tanya said soberly. "I can't imagine. I've never really been on my own. When we moved here, Missy was right next to me all the way."

"I never had nothing like that. I mean, foster life was a lot of getting bounced around, thinking you got somebody, and then they just leave you hanging all the time. Or get you wrapped up in their business so you can't enjoy anything you might want for yourself." He drove on, keeping his composure despite his sullen tone.

Tanya was silent for a few blocks and noticed they were close to her apartment. When Brandt flipped on his signal, she asked, "Mind if we go another way? That's where my car got hit, and I'm kinda still dealing with it."

"No problem. You've been through a lot in a short time too. If you want to talk-"

"I don't think I'm ready for that," she said quickly. "No offense. You're being really sweet, but it's all still fresh, and I feel like I'm still in it."

Brandt nodded without looking over at her. He chewed on his lip as if she had just caught him doing something wrong. "Maybe we could try a real date sometime, not just when you need a ride somewhere?"

She didn't answer as he was parking outside Blush, where she saw Simon's vehicle. She opened the door quickly to get out when Brandt reached out to grab her arm.

"Hey, how about that date? Or at least a thank you?" He pulled her back into the seat as he asked.

Tanya shuddered under his strong grip and slapped at his hand. "What's wrong with you?! I don't owe you shit! Is that why you gave me a ride? To get something from me? What? You thought I was supposed to sleep with you and then thank you?"

She got out of the car and left the door hanging open, then ran up to the club and tested the front door, which she pushed open easily.

Simon stood over Blake's new desk and dropped the pair of purses he brought back for the sisters. "We have a new problem. I won't be long. I'm being followed."

Blake looked at the purses with a raised brow. "What's with the purses? You taking on muggers now?" He rubbed his eyes and face down over his prickly, unshaven chin. "You look like hell."

"Those belong to the girls who were attacked here," Simon said after a heavy breath. "I checked in on their place and found it all ripped apart. The guy who did it got the drop on me, and we tangled."

"Got the drop on you?" Blake asked with surprise. "But you-You're a-"

"Yeah, well, so is he," Simon interrupted. "Anyway, I wanted to bring these back for the girls. But more importantly, I wanted to warn you. Before we fought, he told me those dancers of yours were turned. That all of them are. That he's been watching them and this place for a while."

Blake avoided looking at Simon's face and leaned on his elbows. "You woke me up to tell me my place is infested with vampires, and there's a werewolf doing stakeouts?" He laughed at himself and put his hands up. "Sorry, poor choice of words."

Simon slammed his hands on the desk. "You just can't be serious, can you?"

The sound of squealing tires in the parking lot drew his attention toward the front of the building. He pulled open the office door just as Tanya pushed in on it.

Tanya caught herself with a step and looked between both men in the room. "Uh, hey. Sorry to barge in. The door was unlocked."

"Was that your ride?" Simon asked, looking over her shoulder to the front entrance. "Are you alright?"

"Yeah, long story, but I'm fine," she heaved.

Her face was flushed as she caught her breath. Simon stood

back to give Tanya space to enter the room.

She saw her and Melissa's purses on the desk and grabbed hers. "Well, maybe I don't need to ask now. I was coming to borrow your phone so I can figure out where to buy a new one, but you brought it back." She dug into the clutter and fished out her cellular phone, and the screen flashed long enough to show the battery had died. "Well, that figures. Wait, you guys went in my place to get these?"

Simon drew a breath, but Blake spoke first. "Yeah, well, you said you couldn't go back there, and Simon here wanted to check in on you. He was just telling me what you already said about the break-in. He said the place was thoroughly trashed."

Simon scowled at Blake but softened his expression when she turned to look at him. "I, uh, figured you'd at least want your phone and wallet."

"If it's safe to go back I could use some other stuff. Clothes and my charger, at least. Would you mind?" Tanya leaned on one hip as she rummaged through her purse, checking her wallet. "I can finally throw in some gas money. I'd rather give it to you than a taxi, if that's alright?"

Simon looked over to Blake as he shrugged and then back to Tanya with a nod. "Sure. I'm headed back that way."

She thanked him and pulled her purse strap onto her shoulder. "I just need to check for something I left backstage and I'll be right out."

When she left the room, Blake chuckled and leaned back in his chair. "It's a little early in the day for one of my vampires to be running around ain't it? You said you were followed and then got into a fight. What could someone like that have said that you could trust?"

"I don't even know if I can trust myself. What's with the makeover on this place? Your boss finally decide to spend some money?" Simon asked as he looked out from the door.

Blake stood and smugly replied, "Something like that. After the attack, he and I came to a crossroads. Michael said we should shut it down, but this is all I've got. So he sold it to me. The insurance claim promised to be a chunk, so I made some big changes. What do you think?"

"I think Michael was right," Simon answered without hesitation. "But, you've got people depending on you for income, and putting twenty people out without notice all at once doesn't feel right either. I hope your investment pays off. Keep a watch out, alright? That loose cannon is still out there and has marked this place for bad news. Maybe I can bait him and keep him busy." He turned around, filling the door frame. "We both have our hands full, but we're not done until we find Leila."

Tanya called out from near the entrance, "Are you ready?"

Coming Clean

Tanya wasted no time once Simon started driving. "So you and Mr. Gentry are close or something? Do you work for him?"

She turned herself sideways in the seat, staring at his steely face past a half curtain of messy, sandy hair. He was dressed just the same as last she saw him, though his clothes were muddy, especially his boots. Some mud also clung to the pedals, and chips of it had hardened and lay broken on the floor. She could see his shirt had been ripped open across the chest and carried a heavy sweat stain as if he'd gone for a run on a dirt trail in the rain.

When he didn't answer, she broke the awkward silence. "Looks like we both had a rough night. You didn't get all filthy saving my purse, did you?"

"I don't work for…Mr. Gentry. Blake is my brother. Well, step-brother." Simon didn't return a look to her but frequently checked the mirrors as they drove. "He and I do have kind of a project we're working on."

"Pull over." She finally got his attention and drew his gaze toward her once the jeep was stopped. She jumped out and closed the door to put a barrier between them. "I saw the file. You've been in my business out of nowhere for the last week. Every time I have a problem, you or your brother have been right there, not giving me any answers, and I need to know if

I'm part of your little project."

"It's complicated."

"Yes, or no?" She fixed her eyes on his and waited with an iron grip on the door frame.

"Yes," he confided. "But, you don't understand."

"Then make it crystal clear to me," Tanya demanded. "I can't escape you. I can't get out of this mess I'm in. And I just want to know how much more shit you're going to drag me through!"

"You won't believe me. But I can tell you that if you want to walk away right now, I won't follow you." Simon lowered his face, looking ashamed. "I was trying to keep you safe, and part of that was not telling you."

Tanya narrowed her eyes at him and huffed loudly.

"If you want to know more, get back in. We can at least get your clothes and things before you decide what you want to do, and I'll explain more along the way," Simon offered. "Anything you want to know."

After hesitating, Tanya looked around and huffed again. "Everything. From the beginning."

He nodded reluctantly and gestured to the empty seat. "Everything."

Partway through his explanation, they reached her street, but Simon kept driving. "How badly do you need those things from home? Can we buy some replacements for now? There is still a police patrol watching your place."

"Yeah, I guess so. Keep talking."

The afternoon passed quickly while Simon talked. They ran through her errands, swiping her pre-paid card to buy a charger, some thrift store clothing and shoes, and a drive-thru lunch with extras for later.

"Do you have any idea how crazy this all sounds?" She took a sip from a straw in a large cup. "This is mythical monsters in the real world kind of stuff. How do you expect me to believe all this?"

"I really don't. Which is why I didn't say anything when I stayed to fix your door," Simon explained. "Now I have to ask, what is it you thought any of this had to do with the file you saw?"

She took a minute to choose her words while she chewed and swallowed her bite of burger. "Well, at first, it was just this mess of newspaper clippings, but then I thought about some of the headlines and the missing persons pages I saw. All of what I saw was, 'young woman this,' or 'teenage girl,' that. So I thought the worst, that maybe it had to do with some kind of trafficking to get girls stuck working at the club."

"I told you it was hard to believe," Simon repeated. "We're looking for our sister. We gathered up any reports that might have involved her. She was attacked, much like you were, but turned."

"So if that's what those guys were, why weren't Missy and I turned?" Tanya asked.

"The only thing I could figure was we interrupted them just before." Simon sounded unsure himself. "Then, admittedly, I stayed and watched you at first just to see what would happen when the sun came up. To make sure."

"And you got your proof, so where's mine?" Tanya prodded, "Take me and show me. Teach me what you know, and I can go with you."

"Tanya, wait. It's not that simple." He blew a long breath and pulled into a station for gas. "Some of our leads go cold as fast as they pop up. And everything we encounter is incredibly dangerous, not just to normal people." He re-entered the jeep after pumping and drove toward the outskirts. "The things I've seen I can't just walk away from. Missing children and muggings and murders and all that is horrible enough when regular people do it. But when one of us does it, the lengths a monster will go to to cover their tracks and keep their secrets leave a lot of unresolved resentment from a society that has already lost most of its faith in law and order."

Tanya pressed harder, "I said I want some proof. I think you owe me that. Can you really sit here and tell me you're some kind of shape-changing monster and expect me to just take your word for it?"

"I can't always control it. It's something inside me that's always fighting to get out," he argued. "Any time I want to change, there's a chance it can completely take me over until it's finished with whatever it wants to get or kill. It's a part of me, but I'm just in its way most of the time."

"So? You know what you are. What you're capable of," she added. "How hard can it be to make sure you don't do any harm?"

Simon stomped on the brake pedal and refused to look at her. His mess of hair hid his face as he rested his head on his white knuckles wrapped around the steering wheel.

Tanya held her ribs where the seatbelt yanked against her, but she didn't make a complaint. "Hey. I'm sorry. I've been a pain in your ass all day, and I just… I'm sorry."

"There's just one thing left I think you have a right to know," Simon said through clenched teeth. "I don't have any proof of it. But between what you told me and the car wreck…" Simon looked over at her with a look of pain and regret. "Just like the night I lost my little sister in the subway and I couldn't stop her when she attacked Blake. I thought I was losing all of what was left of my family all over again, and I was only a few steps away from stopping it."

"Wait, you can't be-"

Simon held up a hand, his eyes squeezed shut. "I need you to be quiet for just a minute." He took a few breaths and set his jaw firmly. He rolled his head to stretch the stress in his neck and looked at her again. "Believe me when I say I know this is hard to swallow. We believe Melissa attacked the man who was driving her to the hospital. His throat was torn open, which we think is what caused him to lose control and crash. It was her first feeding as a fledgling vampire. We know she was bitten. We have only Blake's account of pulling the driver from the burning car to be sure she was turned. But I couldn't tell you because you would never have accepted it. You probably still won't."

Tanya's mouth hung open. She looked around them as if nothing was real for a long minute. She pushed her fingers through her hair and stretched her arms up until her hands touched the roof and then punched at it. She kicked at the floor panel and drove her elbow into the door. She screamed through her teeth until it hurt to catch her breath.

Simon got out of the jeep sometime during her angry fit and walked far enough away from her to make a phone call. Tanya had only come down enough from her rage by the time she could see him walking back.

"I'll fill you in when we get there," Simon said into his phone before he flipped it shut.

Mama's Boys

Simon led Tanya out on the concrete expansion on the riverside to a brick maintenance shack where the only door faced the water. He unlocked the door and showed her inside, where they were met with a series of perforated steel stairs. Their steps echoed in the plain, pale gray corridor that took them down under the city, where a network of clearly labeled concrete tunnels hummed around them ever louder as they ventured deeper.

He turned a key in another door labeled MAINTENANCE, then walked them into a room organized with cleaning supplies and stocked lockers of uniforms, gloves, hard hats, face coverings, and an assortment of paint cans.

"Put these on," Simon instructed. "Any time you feel the need to come here, you'll just need to look the part, and no one will bother you for more than a cleanup or bathroom plunge. The people who work the facility clock long hours, and most of them don't like to ask for anything. But if they do, just play along, tell them you'll get right on it, and then make yourself scarce."

He pulled a set of blue overalls out to hand to Tanya with a patch on the chest that read CROSS. "Roll the sleeves and pant legs until it looks like it fits. You can belt the waist with some twine or bring a belt or whatever. The more it looks like it's yours, the less anyone will ask about it."

"Why are we here? Don't tell me you work here?" Tanya asked.

"You don't think I beg my brother for gas money when I come around, do you?" Simon tried to make his question sound like a joke. "I'm not down here a lot. The great thing about a janitor job in a place this big is everybody is too busy to check on your work, and if they run out of toilet paper, they blame it on their wife's cooking instead of me not keeping things stocked. I come down here just enough to keep up appearances, get some pay coming in, and get away from up there when I need to. Come on, there are some people I'd like you to meet."

Further into the facility, Simon brought her to where several dunnage bins were arranged near a door that read HARDHATS REQUIRED. "It can get loud in here, and the chlorine smell is overwhelming at first, but you get used to it."

After securing the door behind them, Simon again took the lead and followed a series of wide blue pipes that stretched and bent along either side of narrow railed walkways through the underworks. Long, parallel, brown pipes hung from the ceiling by U-shaped rebar and spanned the entire length of the stretch in a straight line. Motion sensor lights clicked on along the way until they reached a rectangular vault hatch on one side with a chain hung OUT OF ORDER sign dangling in front of it.

"I'll get you a key to the other doors should you need to come here on your own. But this one could give you some trouble if you're not careful. I jammed the crank so it would be difficult to open for anyone but me. So remember to grab a prybar from the supply office to make it easier on you, and always close the door when you leave."

He took hold of the crank wheel and turned it to the left with a steely groan that echoed loudly against the concrete walls. The heavy door swung in to reveal a lounge area furnished with beaten couches and recliners whose dilapidated cushions sagged with age and wear. A kitchenette and a vending machine partially stocked with salty snacks and microwave meals were in the far corner of the room. Across from the heavy vault door was a ladder leading up into an unlit, circular manhole.

Tanya was startled at the sudden appearance of a black woman also wearing overalls who popped her head out of a side room doorway. Tanya turned to see Simon trying to hide a smile as she stepped back.

"Baby, for a janitor, you sure keep a messy place. Don't you ever clean up for company? You better come over here and give me a kiss, now!" She had a disapproving look on her face that stretched into a broad grin.

Tanya stood near the door as Simon rushed over and picked up the tiny woman in a hug, and spun her around once before putting her back on her feet. Then he leaned down to kiss her as she craned her neck to return it with an exaggerated "MWAH!"

Simon took her hands and pushed the tiny woman a few steps back to look her over. "Time is always so kind to you, Miss Phie. You don't look a day over-"

"No matter what he's about to say, you can be sure it's a pan-fried, saturated fat lie. Nothing but comfort food that only tells the truth when you put your jeans on in the mornin'," Miss Phie said, looking at Tanya. "And don't neither of you dare call me that. You know it makes me feel old. You boys and your new friend here will just call me Mama, as always." She broke free from Simon's handhold and offered her hand to shake to Tanya. "And just who might this little piece of heaven be?"

Simon took a breath, but Tanya beat him to answer. "It's funny you should say. I'm Angel."

"You sure are, sugar. Just look at you! Bright blonde feathers bleached right in the sun itself. Shame to meet a creature so gorgeous in these drab coveralls. What are you doing with this sewer rat? Y'all run into some trouble?" Mama asked.

"More like trouble ran into her. Reno," Simon answered as he pulled his arms out of his overalls and tied the sleeves around his waist.

Mama raised her eyebrows and looked back at Simon. "What did you say to me? What's Reno got to do with this? He's supposed to be long gone."

"Well, he ain't," Simon said flatly. "He trashed Angel's place and then stowed away in my jeep."

Tanya watched dumbfounded as Simon peeled off his shirt, revealing scars on his arms, belly, and chest. Fair, curled hair clung to his defined torso, patterned like an upside-down Christmas tree. His skin had several moles and oddly placed freckles. And when he turned to toss his torn shirt into a trash can, Tanya saw his broad back, which looked like the victim of several whippings, stabbings, and a couple of scars that looked like bullet wounds. She caught her breath and looked at the floor as she crossed her arms uncomfortably until Simon slammed the closet door and pulled a plain, gray shirt from a shelf to put on.

"Sorry if I left that out earlier. We know him. He used to be part of our pack. Speaking of which, I thought Josh was going to be here?"

"He's on his way. He's never been a front door kinda guy. You know that." Mama's voice softened. "You fought with Reno, didn't you? When he stowed on you? I can see it in your eyes. Did you kill that boy?"

Tanya looked hard at Simon, but he only shook his head.

"I don't think so. It's hard to tell for sure. But I legged half a day through the woods in the pouring rain and couldn't find him. That's why I wanted to bring Ta-, Angel down here. Her place is being patrolled by police, and I have to assume Reno is waiting to catch her there alone."

"The whole story from the beginning, huh?" Tanya asked with a dejected tone.

Simon looked surprised at the accusation. "I didn't think it was important at the time to tell you I knew him. Well, I used to, anyway. He's not with us. I told you why he was there. That's what's important. If we intend to get the jump on him, we're going to have to bait him out. He'll likely come to the pack next for sympathy."

"You think he'll come to me licking his wounds because I'm sweet on my boys," Mama confirmed. "I guess that sounds right. But I can't meet him alone. And he knows better than to walk into an ambush."

Tanya and the others looked at the ladder as echoing footsteps descended into the lounge with them.

"And this is our Mr. Joshua," Mama said, nodding toward the ladder. "Late as usual, I see."

Their expected guest turned at the bottom of the ladder with an irritated look on his chiseled face. He was clean-shaven, with a dimpled chin, and his right eye was milk-white with a scar above and below it. He smoothed chesnut curtain bangs out of his face and adjusted his zippered leather jacket with a roll of his shoulders before he approached Tanya directly.

"Haven't been down here in a while," Joshua said as he circled her and smelled her neck. "No need to be afraid, I just like to get a profile. Everyone has their own unique scent."

Mama rolled her eyes at him and threw her hands up as she walked toward the kitchenette. "I told that boy many times, women don't like being SNIFFED! Behave yourself now.

We're not animals! Well, you know what I mean. "

Joshua walked away from Tanya and sat on the arm of a couch facing Simon. "Been doing some hunting, Simon? You still haven't cleaned your gun," he sniffed again. "Or showered recently. You smell like a wet carcass."

"Good to see you too," Simon retorted. "I asked you here for help. Where's Fisher?"

"You know how he feels about closed spaces and inhibiting smells," Joshua said. "I heard everything on the way down. Sound carries in this place like you're passing around a microphone. So, Reno's a problem again? The thing is, we have a little problem of our own. Got a bloomer whose time is coming. It's one thing to play babysitter to one of our own. I'm guessing you brought the girl to meet us, hoping we'd watch her for you?"

"A bloomer? What about the parent?" Simon asked.

"We don't know yet," Joshua said. "I'm just telling you the plate is full."

Tanya stepped forward to make sure she would be noticed when she interrupted. "What's a bloomer?"

Mama shot a sidelong gaze at the men and approached Tanya. "That's what we call the first change. When the moon is bearing down on us, drawing us to her mysteries. It sparks a sort of puberty for a new wolf. Luna, we call her. The moon when she speaks to us at that time, to guide us to the child.

We can sort of feel her intentions, her pull. And we use that to try to find the pup and show them the way so they aren't alone. If the pup accepts us, we will offer a place in our family."

"The first change is difficult to handle. Very few survive it if they have to do it alone," Joshua explained as he and Mama looked at Simon briefly. "And every pack has rivals, so claiming the new wolf can be a matter of war for us. We have to weigh very carefully if a fight is worth trying to save one now or submit to the pup growing to be a rival in the future. There are only a few of us. So when we can, we answer the blooming."

"What does that have to do with this monster following me?" Tanya asked.

"Hey, just as a courtesy among friends, we don't much like being called monsters." Joshua pushed his lips together and cocked an eyebrow. "And, frankly, it has nothing to do with Reno," Joshua replied. "Which is why we can't help you. We'd be looking over our shoulders constantly."

"Oh, 'cause that would be different from any other day, hmm?" Mama broke in. "Mm-hmm. Angel, he's right, though, in this case. We don't have any idea what Reno is planning for you, and our window for the blooming is just one time, one night, that we don't even know for sure when yet."

Simon got up to make coffee, then turned to lean against the sink. "You're right. You shouldn't be taking on any extras right now. At least you've had a chance to meet. So, should you need to come here and find Angel, she's not some stranger, and she's welcome here any time. She needs a place to stay that's safe, and this is it for now."

"We do know what he wants," Tanya corrected. "Simon told me on the way here that he's after vampires."

"Yeah, vampires. He's obsessed." Joshua said. "What's that got to do with anything?"

Tanya uncrossed her arms and confronted Joshua. "Reno thinks I am one. And you just agreed he may come to Mama for help. So what if Mama recruits his help with the blooming in exchange for helping him hunt me?"

Joshua, Mama, and Simon exchanged a look. Mama gave a wink and grinned at Tanya. "You better have one hell of a plan if you expect you and me to be bait, girl. These boys don't let Mama get her hands dirty very often and you're just gettin' your feet wet." Mama put her hand on Simon's shoulder. "I like her. But baby," she looked up at Simon with a condescending shake of her head. "You better dump that coffee right out. It's bad for you, and it stinks to high heaven."

Perishable Goods

Melissa opened her eyes inside what had finally become a familiar four-poster bed with heavy curtains drawn around it. She rose from the mattress to her dark room and made her way out, down the hall in her bare feet and thin satin nightie. She looked about the quiet manor and watched from the top of the staircase as two other residents, whom she had met but couldn't remember their names, left out through the double front doors.

She crept quietly down the stairs despite being told several times to treat this place as a welcome home. Melissa went to the cellar door but hesitantly rested her head against it. She nearly doubled over on weak knees, then grabbed the knob and pulled the door open to descend into the dark below. The lantern Thaddeus used before was hanging in its place near a box of matches on a small, high shelf at the top of the stairs. She struck a match and consciously inhaled to smell the acrid, sulfurous odor, and waited for the sting in her nose that never came. Melissa opened the lantern and lit the wick, tightening the exposure to only what she needed to see ahead.

At the bottom of the steps, she could barely see a short distance around her and tried to maintain a straight line as she moved slowly until she reached the cart of instruments and glassware. The post here was empty, but a faint moaning from deeper into the dark could be heard.

"Is someone there?" Melissa heard a feminine voice pleading.

"Please, will you bring the light closer?"

Melissa moved forward, opening the wick just enough to extend the light until she saw a row of bound people situated far enough from each other that they couldn't reach one another. The first of which was a woman with long blonde hair, a mess all around her face that hung to shoulder length. She was stripped from the waist down, as all the others were. And near each of the people Melissa could see, against the wall, were small matching chamber pots. Melissa could see her pot had tipped over and rolled out of reach.

"Please, I see your light. Can you help me? I don't think I can wait much longer," the woman said. Her voice was cracking and labored.

Melissa set the lantern on the floor and moved closer with slow, careful steps.

"Neither can I," Melissa said as sweetly as she could before throwing her arms around the woman and sinking her fangs into the neck.

The woman moaned as if in pleasure from the bite. Melissa drank deeply, allowing herself to enjoy the privacy of sating her thirst without an audience. A man next to them began to sob loudly in the weak light. Melissa lost her sense of time, not having to leave room to breathe, and continued draining the only drink she would ever need again. She dug her nails into the woman's shirt until the skin underneath tore. The woman's knees went weak, and she hung heavily in Melissa's arms. The room around Melissa began to fade into a haze as she heard a rhythmic beat. Like the ticking of a dull clock getting louder. Getting closer. Until it stopped almost on top of her.

"Miss, I believe that's quite enough," came the voice of Thaddeus behind her. "We must be careful about portions lest we allow hunger to control us."

Melissa let go of the woman, who collapsed to her knees with arms bound by her wrists above her head in chained shackles. Melissa turned to face Thaddeus with a steady stare. "Is this really how you talk all the time? You sound a hundred years old!"

"I speak the way I have always spoken. Clearly, and deliberately," he answered with a hint of a smile. "When I was a boy, this would have been called having a 'stately manner', and as such, I prefer my distinction from today's jibber-jabber."

"I guess that's fair. I don't think I'd be willing to change the way I talk for you either," Melissa admitted. "It just stands out, you know?"

"Then it is as it should be, miss," Thaddeus said with a barely noticeable bow. "Please allow me to tend to this guest of ours. Will you be staying in this evening?"

"I guess so. I don't feel like going out. I don't feel anything." Melissa picked up the lantern and dimmed the light as the man nearby calmed himself to a low whine. "I also noticed some other weird things. Like that dress…well, all the dresses are great, but the peacock gown was amazing. I just wish I could have seen myself in it, you know?"

The row of other bound guests had also become restless since Melissa and Thaddeus had begun speaking.

Thaddeus pressed a pair of fingers to the bound woman's neck and gently touched her face. "You almost ended this woman's life, which is why we prefer to use our tools to ration how much we take at a time. I will be happy to assist you in the future, so we might be more careful of over-indulgence."

"Thaddy, I-"

"Thaddeus, miss, is quite familiar enough if you please?"

"Okay, sorry," Melissa forced an apology. "Thaddeus. I don't get the point of this. These people are-"

He interrupted again. "Ah. Speaking of our guests as though they aren't present is impolite. Upstairs, please."

When they reached the top and hung the lantern, Thaddeus closed the door and began to answer. "Those people are under my care. They have come to us willingly and received the hospitality they each requested. Reprieve from the cold and hunger of living on the street. They had each an opportunity to leave once they had the warmth and meal they had hoped for, and each overstayed their welcome. Therefore I offered an extended stay and promised they would never suffer the cold nights of our lonely city outside these walls." He held up a hand when Melissa looked like she might interrupt him. "Our existence here at Valiant is unnatural, to say the very least. We have requirements to meet each day for quite a sum of residents. Thankfully, most nights, Master Fletcher's family members prefer to go choose for themselves and retain a place among society in some respects. But we'd be remiss not to ensure a healthy, ready supply of libations."

They had ascended the curved staircase back up to her room, where Thaddeus entered with Melissa and addressed the mirror. "The blood, or vitae, as Mr. Fletcher prefers, is what allows you to wake from your slumber each night. You use what you imbibe to carry out many tasks, and is the cost of any gift you may have within you. There are limits, of course, but it is the price that you pay for immortality. You must be patient, and deliberate, and your gifts will show themselves to you in time."

He gestured to the mirror at her vanity, where Melissa took a seat. She looked hard at the mirror as she had done several times since the start of her new life. As she focused her gaze on the glass, she pulled her hair in front of one shoulder and stroked the length of her straight brown locks. The empty room in the reflection was soon blocked by her own face. She watched as Thaddeus placed a hand on her pale shoulder. Melissa smiled at herself, then curled her tongue and touched her cheeks.

She only stopped for a moment when Thaddeus turned to leave. "One is glad to be of service, miss."

Blake unrolled the tape on his wrists and removed a pair of padded gloves while the heavy bag hanging from his loft rafter was still swinging toward neutral on its three-point chain. Sweat dripped into his eyes and down over his bare, freckled chest to the soaked waistband of his workout pants. His phone vibrated with an obnoxious jingle on the nightstand, heavily enough to walk itself to the edge of the table. He caught the phone just before it fell and unlocked the screen to reveal a new message from Leila.

"I gotta pick a shorter tone for that. Or level this table," he said out loud to himself.

"Here's the ad for the showcase I've been planning. It's the perfect time to send your girls up to meet me for their big audition. Don't disappoint me like Michael did."

CREATURES OF THE DARK
BARE YOUR SOULS

ONE NIGHT ONLY
BLACK FRIDAY MIDNIGHT
LADY CLEO IN THE FLESH
LIVE FEEDING ON CENTER STAGE

CAPACITY LIMIT
PRE-ORDER NOW!

Blake forwarded the ad to Angel's number, then a separate one to Rose. Their numbers were still saved under their stage names, as he had with all his girls at Blush.

When he sent Angel's message, he added, "Dress nice. Cleo says it's more like an audition than an interview. She wants to see your style. Be there a few hours before the big show at midnight."

Rose's message was different. Blake chose his words carefully. "Might be a hell of an opportunity for you to make a name for yourself outside of a sister act. Tell Cleo I sent you."

Blake tossed his phone on his unmade bed and stripped, leaving his pants on the floor as he went to start the shower.

Blindsided

"No, Mom, I don't think so," Tanya said into her phone. "There's just a lot to juggle, and I don't think I'll come back to finish school if I come home. Sorry, the reception here isn't great. What did you say?"

Tanya paced the underground lounge after stripping off the overalls. She didn't dare to remove her shoes in the unfamiliar place.

"Mom, it's not that I need to be convinced. I just- No, you don't need to put Daddy on I-" Tanya huffed in defeat and tried to sound as sweet as she could. "Hi, Daddy. No, I'm alright. Just. You know how things can pile up when you're trying to do it all. No, Missy's not here. She never is anymore." She caught her tone changing to anger and calmed herself. She sat on the musty recliner and bent over with her head in her hand.

"Well, yeah, we had a fight about some job stuff, but nothing we can't handle. She made some new friends and has been hanging out with them more. And so have I, actually." She sat up and looked around at the mostly empty walls. "No, like just some people I met for help on a… A project that's due soon. What? No! I do not have a boyfriend. I don't have time for that right now, Daddy. Right. Well, it's just one more semester. And I have a job interview coming up too. I think it's an internship or something, which would be perfect to add to my resumé. It's some kind of smaller designer just getting her name out. It looks like she's been out a few years but not competing in the big leagues yet."

Tanya nodded to her father, even though he couldn't see. "Yeah. I keep telling her to call you. She's just. Well, you know. Okay, I will. I love you too, Daddy. Tell Mom for me, too, okay? Okay, bye."

She opened her text messaging app on the screen and tapped on Melissa's picture, but there were no new messages. She took another look at the ad and message Blake sent her late last night. Her thumbs flew across the keyboard on-screen to send a reply. She pulled on the large overalls again and made her way to the door to leave through the tunnels.

The message read, "I need a ride, and we need to talk. The creep that's after me is watching the club. I'll get you an address in a few minutes."

"It's been a while since I've taken a night off, but I'm confident you guys can handle things here," Blake said to Brandt and the security team before opening time. "With everything up to date, it should be easier than ever to be a little short-handed. You guys know what to do. Doors open in twenty minutes, plenty of time to bring the girls in and do all your checks. It's not likely to be too busy. You'll barely notice I'm gone. Just a reminder, no phones out on the floor. Don't get lazy on me."

Brandt dismissed the other men with a nod and waited until

they were a few steps away before asking Blake for a chat in his office.

"You could have given us a better heads up, boss. Don't you usually want a couple of hours for a call-off?" Brandt paced in front of the door, fidgeting with his hands.

Blake reached into the top drawer of his desk for a pair of gloves and zipped up his jacket. "I thought the guys would all prefer to hear it directly since they know I live upstairs. Didn't want everybody on edge if I was just a no-show. But I don't want everybody too relaxed just because I'm out either. Good for morale, right? And I need you to keep a tight ship while I'm gone."

Brandt nodded and tried to show some confidence. "I just ain't used to the responsibility yet, I guess. But everybody needs a night off, boss, I get it."

"Sometimes, the best way to learn how to be the boss is to get thrown to the wolves." Blake checked his phone and gave Brandt a playful slap on the arm. "Try not to burn the place down."

Blake left the office, took another look around the club, then grabbed his motorcycle helmet from behind the bar. The parking lot was still quiet, with the last girls being escorted inside with a bouncer through the back door. He threw a leg over his bike and let the engine growl while strapping his helmet into place. He set the gear and drove off across town to the address in Tanya's message.

Blake parked in front of a small diner near the waterfront and saw Tanya sitting inside at a booth. He pulled his helmet off as the nearby firehouse siren bleated into the evening air. When he walked inside, the older waitress hollered at him to close the door.

"All that noise out there! Sorry handsome, it just echoes in here something awful. Can I get you something?" the waitress asked with a smoker's lilt.

"Uh, just a coffee, thanks," Blake answered as he went to sit with Tanya.

"I'm not gonna mess around here," Tanya started before Blake settled into his seat. "This guy chasing me is an old friend of your brother's. Well, he was. They had a fight and now Simon's out chasing him down and left me sitting on my hands."

"Sounds like Simon has his hands full. His old friends are… well-"

"I know what they are. And I know a lot more than that. But I want you to fill in the blanks."

Two fire engines screamed by the diner window, and the street light flickered outside. Blake and Tanya watched together as the trucks parted traffic.

"Here's your coffee, hon." The waitress said, and Tanya jumped in surprise. "Sorry, sweetie. You sure you don't want anything?"

The cook peeked out to the dining room to see if any orders were coming back. "Hey Margie, you know any of the girls work down at that strip club? It's on the scanner."

"I told you, turn that thing off when I'm working. I hate all that. Nothing but bad news," Margie answered.

"Hey, sorry, it keeps me occupied," the cook shrugged.

"What was on the scanner?" Tanya asked the cook.

The cook leaned into the ready window. "That nudie club. That's the fire call."

"Oh, my god. Missy!" Tanya cried out.

Blake flipped a five-dollar bill on the table next to his untouched coffee and shot up out of his seat for the door. When he got out to his motorcycle, Tanya was right behind him. "Put this on quick," he said, tossing his helmet to her.

Tanya barely had her hands clasped around Blake's belly when he cranked the throttle and tore off toward Blush. When they took the next turn toward the club, he could see the plume of smoke in the air and the bright, spinning red lights of the fire engines.

Before they reached the crowd gathered around the burning building, Blake saw a large dog run into the road and stop right in front of him. He squeezed the brake hard but didn't have enough room to stop as the bike fish-tailed with a squeal of rubber. The animal lay down just before Blake collided with enough momentum to flip him and Tanya over the handlebars into the road. He could feel Tanya still holding tight and tried to brace the fall with both arms in front of his face. Tanya slipped up his back upon impact, and he could hear her helmet slamming into the pavement. Blake rolled over to get to his feet when the large dog pounced on his chest and made his head hit the hard road beneath him. The snarling beast growled closely into his face, then spun and wavered as Blake struggled to stay conscious from the blow to his head.

"Simon…she asked me to. I tried to just send her away… Simon," Blake slurred and mumbled, and the world went dark.

It's a Long Story

Simon dropped his keys on a table inside the door of the community cabin. He closed the door when the others were inside.

"I missed this place," Simon said as he looked around the familiar fixtures.

An upstairs balcony with log rails overlooked the main living space. In the center of the room was a pool table with felt worn bare in several places. Church pew-style benches lined the room's walls, and a travel television sat on a buffet counter that split the room from a rustic wood stove kitchen. The other surrounding cabins were once used as dormitories for children and teens for summer camps and boy scout retreats. The simple log-built walls went undecorated.

Fisher, Joshua, and Mama stood anxiously in the room. Fisher scratched at the blond scruff growing on his chin, then pushed a hand through his springy hair. He was tall and thin, with cord-muscled arms exposed from his sleeveless metal band t-shirt.

Fisher asked in a baritone voice as his throat bobbed a prominent Adam's apple, "Are you sure we should go on a hunt right now? Exposing our hunting habits to Reno leaves Mama a sitting duck. Do you think he'll remember that I always go out just before a new moon?"

"That's the whole point, baby," Mama said. "I thought we explained that to you. Reno would never hurt me. If you recall, I voted that he stay, and he'll remember I told him he could come to me if he had any trouble. I just wish the circumstances were different. It's one thing to let someone go. But to set him up feels so shitty."

Joshua looked hard at Simon. "We don't have to do any of this. But I don't want Reno running around making new problems for us either."

Simon put his hands up. "This isn't an execution. It's more like an intervention. Once we have him on board with Mama's trust, we put him on a goose chase, and we just happen to know where it leads. We can surround him and give him an ultimatum there. The worst part is, if we're wrong about him coming here, we'll have wasted another half tank of gas and a holiday. Which reminds me," Simon added. "What are we hunting?"

Fisher seemed glad to talk about something else. "As always, there are plenty of deer out this way. And they make for a longer hunt with their land speed and put up no fight. It's the best-calculated decision for buying time. We'd likely be out most of the night. And they'd take us a few miles out at least. Anything else is just a matter of burrows and dens if you want something a bit scrappier."

"No, deer is perfect," Joshua chimed in. "No need to exhaust ourselves with any kind of actual fight. We need to be able to get back quickly if things don't work out here."

Mama crossed her arms in front of Simon as he went toward a bench. "Don't you be sitting on the furniture spreading your scent around the place too much. I need Reno to trust me. And I need all of you to trust me with him too. Take your jeep and get these boys outta my house for a while. I'll take care of things here. Y'all just have a good hunt now. And bring me back some mushrooms. That'll keep you out a bit longer, and let me do some cooking for a change. I'm in the mood for a stew." Mama looked into Simon's eyes closely. "And when you get on your way back to town, pick up a present for that nice girl you left all alone waiting. She's scared and got nobody to hold her in that cold dungeon where you left her. Now go on."

Simon gave an understanding nod and picked up his keys to go outside. Their drive went on for nearly an hour, leading them further into the woods, eventually off any kind of road where his vehicle could be better hidden among the dense trees.

Fisher stretched his legs from the cramped space of the back seat as he stood up. "I'm almost certain no matter how this goes, I'll be glad to walk back to the cabin."

"Relax. You could have jumped out and run alongside at any time," Joshua joked. "Probably could have got here long before us."

Simon's phone chirped a ringtone with a banner that read Tanya. "Yeah? You okay? What do you mean? I told you to stay- Nevermind, I'm on my way. What are you doing out there? Alright. Stay put." He closed the flip phone and turned the key in the ignition. "Some other time, boys. Happy hunting."

"Is it that girl?" Joshua asked.

"My brother wrecked his bike. He's torn up. I gotta go," Simon explained.

"You have a brother?" Fisher asked. "Since when?"

"It's a long story. Remind me to tell you sometime when all this is over," Simon said as he shifted into reverse.

"Miss," Thaddeus began. "Master Fletcher would like to meet with you alone tonight to make a proper introduction, as he intended before the ball. He sends his apologies for the delay." Thaddeus held a deep blue box that was slightly larger than both of his hands.

"Another dress?" she asked. "My closet is full already. Does this guy ever get tired of spending money?"

"You'll find Master Fletcher enjoys giving gifts," Thaddeus replied. "Though in this case, he instructed that you open this box in front of him. I'll escort you to him now."

Melissa looked at her phone again and saw only one message from Mr. Gentry that she hadn't opened, but nothing new from Tanya. She pushed her hands up into her hair to fan it out from the flat look her extra time in bed had created.

"Yeah, okay, I guess," Melissa said. "Hey, I was wondering about this place. Has anyone ever decided not to stay? Like your guests in the cellar. They clearly don't want to be here anymore but aren't free to go. Am I free to go? And if so, would I be welcome back? Or is it kind of like the Amish, and you get one chance to try things out, but if you come back, it's forever?"

"Perhaps you could ask Master Fletcher about that, miss," Thaddeus answered. "His children are expected to follow the rules of his home."

Melissa stared hard at Thaddeus, almost interrupting him. "The rules of the house were never explained to me. It's just been gifts, and-and parties, and this huge quiet place and this emptiness inside of me. I feel more like I've been bought than invited. No. That's not true. I don't feel that. I don't feel anything. I don't even miss things I used to do. I just think about it like a story somebody told me. Like the life I was living just a week ago is ancient history now. I mean, it's nice to not need anything. But what about when I used to want something? There's no purpose in any of this… This so-called life. This endless cycle. What about you? What do you want? Don't you ever just want to go home?"

Thaddeus returned her gaze and chose his words. "My home is here, miss. If there is somewhere else you'd like to be, it would be my pleasure to take you there, as always. However, I advise you to meet with Master Fletcher before you depart. Get the answers you seek before resigning yourself to a world outside that doesn't understand."

"Fine then," she said. "Let's go meet him. Anything is better than just sitting here waiting to be told what to wear and who to dance with. I can't even sit and be miserable when misery has been erased from me."

Thaddeus escorted Melissa down the hallway and up another flight of stairs to the master bedroom. He knocked quietly but firmly, and the door opened a moment later.

Melissa watched as the door opened to reveal a man not much taller than herself, barefoot and only wearing relaxed-fitting black pants. He held the same golden knight mask in front of his face long enough for her to see, then pulled it away to show a broad smile. The man's face was angular, with a square chin. He looked at her with bright brown eyes, almost veiled by a mess of black hair.

"Welcome, little flower," he spoke with a thick Eurasian accent. "Please, come inside." He took the box from his servant with gratitude and relieved him. "Enjoy the rest of your evening, Thaddeus."

"Thank you, sir." Thaddeus gave each of them a nod and left them.

"I must apologize for my delay in meeting you formally. I would not want my children to think I don't value their place in my home. You may, of course, call me Atticus."

Melissa swatted the blue box out of his hands across the floor as Mr. Fletcher's gaze followed it in whimsical disappointment. The lid flipped open, and a piece of silvery jewelry that looked large enough to cover a cocktail dress lay in a twist of thin chains in the tissue paper.

"I'm not a flower. And I'm not your child," Melissa began coldly. "This place certainly doesn't feel like a home. It's just a big, cold, empty place. I never see anyone but your butler. And the first time I could have met any of them, you were all wearing masks and pushing me to-"

"Slow down, please." Atticus held up his hands and put his mask down on a small table near his poster bed. Its dark curtains were drawn open, and his bed was topped with a colorful Persian rug rather than a proper blanket. "I understand this is still a strange place to you. I distantly recall what it was like as a child unable to rest peacefully in a new home. Hearing every floorboard. Seeing every shadow. Tree branches tap on the windows, threatening to break the glass and invite the storm inside."

Melissa avoided his face. Instead, she looked around at the crystal chandelier that hung above them and the unlit silver candlesticks in the arched windows. She stepped closer to an immense impasto painting on the far wall that featured a family portrait with the background of a palace. The figures stood at the middle platform of a grand staircase adorned with a bright red carpet with gold trim.

"What about the night I came here?" Melissa asked. "The night I became… this."

"Please, do not fear what we are," Atticus chided softly. "We are vampires. That which can wake only during the night.

We who capture life only by stealing it from others. And that which flows now through our veins grants us gifts that a natural life never could. Unimaginable power that becomes as simple as a snap of fingers. "

"Power and gifts, huh?" Melissa nodded and finally looked at his face again. "Things I never asked for. I barely even got a chance to start figuring out what kind of life I wanted. And in the snap of your fingers, I lost all that."

"What have you lost, little flower? Hmm?" Atticus stared across the room at her. "Lost selling yourself to men who appreciate you only for your fleeting beauty? Lost battling the cold weather for your health? Lost the worry of cancer? Lost the fear of sexually transmitted diseases? Lost the pressure to be the kind of woman society desires that will someday be reduced to nothing more than a housewife? Or captive in a lonely career path that consumes all the time and money it takes to be successful in exchange for your carefully planned illusion of happiness? Perhaps you think you have lost the ability to occasionally escape all of that for a rare quiet vacation weekend on a beach, sipping mind-warping drinks while some boy rubs oil on your skin, only to return to a life you lie to yourself about every day being the best version of you that you could ever be for your efforts?" Atticus disappeared in a mist of shadow and whispered into her ear from just over her shoulder. "Did you truly desire to painfully walk through all of that, slowly year by year, only to work your way toward a goal such as this place filled with any comfort you could ever desire, to then realize that you have become too old and tired to enjoy any of it?"

Melissa stood still and closed her eyes. "I didn't ask for this. The problem is you didn't ask me. This was not my choice. You've taken something you can't give back! There's no ribbon-wrapped box you can hand to me with my life in it for me to open whenever I want."

Atticus stepped around her so quietly that she didn't know he was in front of her until she opened her eyes.

"Very well. All of this is true. And now you are here, in my care," Atticus nodded seriously. "So I will make you an offer that should have been made to you before you were embraced."

"Attacked," Melissa cut in.

"As you wish to say," he continued. "Something you should know before accusing me another time is that I did not choose you. I did not snap my fingers to change you. And the business that drew me away from meeting you before was finding out who it was who did so." He turned from her with his hands behind his back and paced toward the table where his gold mask lay. "However, as that makes me a sort of foster parent to you, if you'll have me, my offer is simple. You may stay here as long as you like and enjoy the life we live secretly in this city. And you may, of course, ask anything of me. Whether it is a favor, a home of your own, or information. Anything you desire. But each of these comes with a price. These things you ask will come in exchange for drawing you closer to me into a bond that is unbreakable. A bond you will feel that reminds you that you belong to me. To perform my will as I desire. If you ask nothing of me, your freedom is your own, and so long as you respect my house, you are welcome here anytime hereafter. Do you understand?"

"So, if I ask who attacked me, I start some kind of obligation to you?" she asked. "If I want Thaddeus as my own personal servant, what? I sell my soul to you?"

"It is not your soul that interests me, little flower," Atticus answered. "But in this house, we must understand that gifts I offer freely are my choice. And the value of choice is something you clearly understand on a profound level. So when you wish for something that costs me, I simply ask that cost be repaid. And, if you so choose to ask me for something you could spend your time doing on your own, such as investigating your crime, securing a palace for your own, or making a peaceful future with your family, you will owe that debt to me. Absolutely. As I command, when I command. All of these things you are quite capable of on your own, of course. So you will weigh the price of your wishes very carefully."

Melissa looked back at the painting again, at the place where it showed a young girl near the edge of the picture. She was beside a garden at the bottom of the stairs in a white dress with a blue ribbon wrapped around her waist. The girl was close to a broad iron gate, waving at someone reaching through from the other side.

"What will it cost me to ask who she is?"

"Now, that is a story you could not possibly find on your own," Atticus answered. "A freely shared story, if you will. Firstly, I had the painting made to recreate a photo that was fading and lacking in color. Parts of it were blurred, cracked, and torn. But as to your question, Calla is my youngest sister. Locked away in an asylum from my family at the end of that summer. She was ill-tempered and strong-willed. Calla did not see her 14th birthday with the family. After her hand was promised to the son of a wealthy family, the boy tried to take advantage of her. She fled him from the stables and trampled him to near death on her horse. He lived to a miserly old age with many wives, but no heir to his fortune. Calla was locked away for defending herself. Confined to a prison disguised as a mental hospital, where I would visit as often as my father would allow. She told me often that she was tortured in the name of saving her sanity. It drove me mad to be unable to rescue her."

Atticus looked over the details of the painting, touching the layered contour in the garden and the dress ribbon. "When my father died of a rare case of croup, I was soon met by a man who offered me the life you see. I knew quickly that time would soon cruelly take my Calla from me, and so I took a piece of my inheritance to go have Calla's papers put in order and shared my gift with her as well.

"It was selfish of me," he continued. "And I thought I knew what was best for her. But she, like you, did not want this gift. She ran from me to the cliffs where we once played and dreamed together. We'd watch the shaping clouds above and ships sailing by, far away from the waves that crashed on the sharp rocks below. It was there that she fled in the latest hours of the dark, just before the sun would touch the horizon. To preserve myself, I hid away from the light. But before I did, I saw her throw herself from the cliff.

"Our kind might be able to survive such a fall, but certainly not the morning sun." Atticus turned, and addressed Melissa directly. "And so afterward, I purchased the asylum and saw to its conversion to a more modern hospital, whose purpose would be for rehabilitation and not just to hold shamed castaways until they died from abandonment."

"That's a hell of a story," Melissa said, finally looking at the man before her, comparing to his likeness in the painting. "Who is that reaching through the gate?"

"That's Calla," he pointed. "She could not stand still for the photograph and was asked to leave. The girl in the garden is our sister between. Danica. She could not be torn so far away from her sister for even a few minutes and was allowed to go as far as the garden so as not to spoil the portrait. Danica was thrown from the very horse that trampled Calla's betrothed on the same day Calla was sent away. She did not survive the fall. This painting is my most valuable possession."

Bumps in the Night

Tanya redialed Melissa's number, but it only rang until reaching voicemail. After the beep, she spoke with a huff, "Missy, I need you to call me back." She sent a text that read, "Please tell me you aren't at work!" Then another that read, "Don't ignore me. I need to hear from you ASAP!!"

A young Hispanic man that introduced himself as Mo looked up at her from where he sat next to Blake on the floor. He had already cut open the pant leg of Blake's jeans to check for any breaks in the skin and had started to duct tape two wooden legs he unscrewed from a small table against either side of Blake's knee.

"Why did you bring us here instead of the hospital?" Tanya asked.

"I already told you, I know this guy. He don't like hospitals. How long have you known him?" Mo asked.

"I dunno. A couple of months. We work together," Tanya said. "I don't know that much about him."

"Hey, no judgment," Mo said defensively. "I want to get this boot off him, but if his ankle is broke that ain't gonna help him none. He nearly punched me out when I put weight on it, and then he blacked out again."

"You never told me how you got him in your car," Tanya said.

"And why are we in this apartment?"

She couldn't help but notice the pictures all over the place and how clean it was, aside from the overstuffed trash can. The dining table, only big enough for two, had cloth placemats and a tall jar candle in the center against the wall. The kitchen was small, and the brown, dented refrigerator didn't appear to fit in its space below wallpapered cabinets. Tanya looked back to Mo and couldn't help but notice he had a bruise on his forehead in an almost perfect circle the size of a paper towel roll. She looked away from Mo to Blake's helmet on a nearby chair with the impact damage just above the broken visor, then back to Blake lying on the linoleum kitchen floor.

"Leather slides on pavement like a tarp on wet leaves. Bikers don't wear that stuff just to look cool, you know? The tough part was getting his legs inside to close the door," Mo answered. "It's my sister's place. She's a nurse and should be home any minute." Mo bit through the tape and pulled it tight to stick it into place. "Can you get me some ice? There should be some sandwich bags or something in one of the drawers."

Tanya opened the freezer to find an ice pack for a lunch cooler and brought it back to Mo. "This should work, right?"

"Oh, nice. Feel up his leg real gentle for the warmest spot, and tape that on over the pant leg." Mo grabbed the tape roll again and bit off two lengths. "How's your head, chica? Your helmet took most of the shot, but you can't be too careful."

The front door slammed shut, and a light clicked on in the hallway. "Gilly, you better not have been in a fight again!" The voice from down the hall was feminine and full of anger.

Mo stood up and went to greet the woman, but she came into the doorway before he could and pushed him out of the way. "Who are these people? Did he get shot?"

"No, Gia, I told you I don't roll with that kind of crew," Mo responded apologetically. "He got hit off his bike, and he and I go back a bit. She was riding on back and got a bump on her head. She said her arm hurts too. What was your name again?"

"Uh, Angel. And this is Blake," Tanya answered as she crossed her arms.

"Gilly, this ain't a free clinic. First, you get a knot on your head during some street fight. Now you're bringing people into my home?!" Gia threw her hands around in wide gestures and tossed her purse on the empty chair at her dining table. "Don't even talk to me about your crew. I know you been carrying a gun. You're lucky I got off work on time tonight," she said as she dropped to one knee to get a closer look at Blake's leg. "Nice splint job on the leg, pendejo. Is that my key table taped to him?"

"Yeah, I had to think fast. It might just be a twist," Mo explained. "I couldn't see no swelling, but his leg felt hot and he couldn't walk on it. Might even be the ankle. The legs on that table screw loose, so I can make it right after."

Gia pulled the ice pack up to look for any swelling and pressed her hand in several places under the torn pant leg of

Blake's jeans. "I think you got a few screws loose. Whatever, this isn't too bad for a motorcycle accident. How long has he been unconscious?"

"About an hour, I think," Mo answered. "How'd you know it was a bike accident?"

"Your girl here is staring at a busted helmet, and there are road rash frays on his leather. Why didn't you text me or something so I could bring home supplies?" Gia asked, not looking up from the splinted leg.

Mo replied with a defensive tone. "Because you just gonna tell me no, and don't bring no troubles in your house."

"That's the smartest thing you've said in years, Gilly. But you brought them anyway, hmm?" Gia snarked back and then looked up at Tanya. "And what about you, honey? Angel, was it? How's your head? Are you having any pain or trouble moving your neck? You said your arm hurts." She stood and placed her fingers on either side of Tanya's jaw to guide her gently.

Angel barely noticed she was being spoken to until the nurse touched her face. "I, uh, I think my arm is fine. Just feels like it got slammed in a door." Tanya moved slowly with Gia's hands to roll her head through a range of motion. "My neck's a little sore to turn to the left, and I'm getting a headache."

"Alright, Angel. A name to match the face, huh? Let me wash up and see if I have some gloves and get some wipes or something for you," Gia said as Tanya started to sob. "Hey,

hey. Honey, it's okay. Accidents happen. We're gonna do the best we can, okay? I think your boyfriend needs to check in at a hospital, but only if he goes by ambulance because I don't want to upset this leg or his head too much."

Tanya could barely see through burning tears and looked up at the spinning shadows from the ceiling fan casting over a statuette of the Virgin Mary on a decorative wooden wall shelf.

"I just…we were on our way to where I work when the diner radio scanner said there was a fire." Her words ran together in a thick jumble as Tanya struggled to breathe. "And my sister works there too with, like, twenty other people. And I just don't understand what's happening."

"Come on with me and just sit down a minute," Gia said as she took a gentle hold of Tanya's arm with one hand and wrapped the other carefully around her back. "Even if it had been just the wreck, it can be a lot to take. All that at once is gonna eat you up. Just try to relax, and we'll get you back outta here so you can find out what's happening, okay? Right now I can't give you answers to anything but what's right here in front of me."

"Gianna!" Mo whispered excitedly. "I think he's coming around."

Tanya was surprised by Blake sitting upright suddenly and shouting with a wide swing of his right arm that barely missed Mo. "Pull the trigger, you little shit!" Blake's eyes were open but showing mostly the white portions as his face flushed bright red.

Gia moved toward Blake outside his reach and tried to look at the back of his head. She shot a look at Mo, "No gun problems, huh? Hold still, now. You're gonna be okay. You took a big bump on the head and need to let me take a look, okay?"

Blake's eyes opened wider at the sound of Gia's voice. "Who is that? You don't sound like one of my girls. MY GIRLS!" Blake looked directly at Tanya as she stood up in front of him.

Tanya tried to wipe her eyes quickly and sound reassuring. "Hey, I'm right here, okay? We're getting you some help, and then we can go check-"

"No! We gotta go now!" Blake tried to shout, but his voice was barely above a whisper as he shook his head and raised a hand to hold where it hurt.

Gia brushed her fingers across his hair near the impacted area and Blake groaned. "I think your head is gonna hurt a few days, and you shouldn't be driving anywhere. Think you can tell me about how this leg feels?"

Blake blinked hard a few times and looked at his leg wrapped in tape. "I need to get up. Just gotta walk it off."

Gia put a hand on his shoulder. "Right now I just want you to try to bend your knee and rotate your ankle and tell me how it feels. One thing at a time. If it feels alright, we can try walking on it."

Tanya looked over to Mo, who was still sitting out of Blake's reach, almost behind him. "How do you know him? You said he would refuse a hospital earlier."

Mo stood up, shook his head and dipped his chin downward before looking into her eyes. "Listen, I gotta come clean, 'cause you really should let him go to a doc. I was following him. Your friend here, I mean. He and I fought a couple days back, and he gave me this." Mo pointed up to his forehead. "I was-"

"He tried to rob me, and I gave him a reason not to," Blake chimed in. "Yeah, I remember you." Blake turned himself on the floor to put his back against the wall and held his throbbing head for his trouble.

Gia stared at Mo and punched his shoulder hard. "What were you thinking, Guillermo? Robbery? I told you to clean yourself up!"

"Gia, I didn't take nothing. And he got me good with just one shot. I'm done with that, okay? OKAY?" Mo made himself stand up straight and look at his sister's face. "I ain't proud of it. And I'm done. But I need to show them something. I saw who torched that place. Got it recorded on my phone."

"You robbing me for a couple of bucks, but you can afford a camera phone?" Blake asked.

"Hey, come on, wey. Phones ain't all expensive. Nobody in

this hood gotta drop a G on something gotta be replaced every couple years, you know?" Mo pulled his cell phone from his back pocket and tapped the screen before turning it around. "I saw the guy who torched that strip club. I called it into 9-1-1 as I was recording, and I think he was the same asshole who popped you off your bike. I saw him run off after I heard the bike go down. He was sniffing you or something when he heard me holler at him. You ain't gonna believe me, but I could swear he turned into some kind of dog or something. You know, like a big one. But when I blinked, he was a man again, and he ran off."

The others watched the footage on the phone screen, and Tanya doubled over when the man in the video bent something around the door handles from the outside. The boarded doors revealed nothing inside the club, and a moment later, an explosion went off as the mostly bald man with a scar across his scalp ran off-screen.

Gia helped Tanya get out the back door to the porch, where she promptly threw up into the grass. Tanya screamed out with her nose and mouth dripping into the grass. "BUT WHY THOUGH? WHY US?"

In her back pocket, Tanya's phone vibrated and jingled a musical tone.

Gia asked, "Angel, do you need me to get that for you?"

Tanya didn't answer the nurse but heard her snap off a rubber glove as she pulled the phone from Tanya's pocket. "Honey, it's someone named Simon calling you. Is that somebody you need to talk to right now?"

"What were you doing there?" Blake asked coldly. "You following me?"

"Hey man, you got me good. I was looking to get some back," Mo explained. "But I ain't want to torch your place or nothin'. Just want to get you scared or whatever and then saw that guy."

"Well, not that it matters, but I don't scare easy, in case you hadn't learned that from the gas station." Blake laughed. "You got a smoke? I tried to quit, but something tells me that's not gonna happen now."

"Nah, man, sorry," Mo shook his head. "Hey, you want to try putting weight on that leg?"

"If I can trust you not to pull a gun on me again," Blake joked. "Yeah, give me a hand."

Mo helped pull Blake up from the floor. Blake took a few steps and winced a little at first. "It'll be fine. Must have tweaked my ankle on the fall. But it doesn't hurt too bad. You mind cutting off the tape? I got a knife in the other boot there."

Mo pulled a butterfly knife from his pocket and fanned it open.

"You're gonna hate me saying this, but you're kind of a textbook example of a juvie kid." Blake laughed again. "Maybe you'll meet my brother someday. He looks like an upgraded backwoods version of you, especially walking around the city. Why aren't you working somewhere to help your sister pay some bills instead of running the streets for small gains."

Mo pulled apart the tape and set the table legs aside, then shrugged. "The crew I run with now takes some weird jobs. Stuff that don't add up in the papers, you know? Boogeyman, vigilante-type stuff. It sounds crazy, but we've seen some things we can't explain, and most of what we do ain't legal. My guys just need a little help with funding once in a while for ammo, or vehicles, or equipment. A stick-up sounded like some quick, easy money, and those little podunk stations are insured to the hilt. Besides, I ain't nobody in that part of town. I tried the jobs I could get for a while, and it's just a hassle. Stuck in one spot, doing the same shit day after day for some disrespectful old white dude telling me I ain't ever gonna be nothin', you know? How long is a guy just tryna make some paper supposed to put up with that?"

"I guess I can relate to some of that," Blake said. "I caught a lucky break real early. My first job wasn't anything special, but my boss treated every little thing I did like it was some really important job. Moving boxes around, unpacking trucks, parking cars. Just, every little thing I did seemed to make him so proud. Something I never really had before then."

"That part I get. The old man was hard on you, huh?" Mo walked out the back door with Blake to check on the girls.

"Mine was pretty tough. Some days you just wanna shoot 'em, you know? If only."

"Yeah. If only."

Headlights flashed across the yard as a jeep turned around in front of the house. Gia looked up and asked Blake, "Is this your ride? It's pretty late for anybody else."

Blake shielded his eyes until the flash went by. "Yeah, I think so. How did he find us so fast, though?"

"Your girl's been on the phone since we got in the car," Mo replied. "It's good to have a crew you can call when shit hits the fan."

Blake looked back to Mo. "What do you say we call it even between us? This bump on my head is probably gonna last as long as yours." He held out a hand to shake with Mo.

"I can respect that," Mo shook his hand. "Hey, you want me to send that video to you? Maybe you can get a better look at that guy?"

"Yeah, sure." He huffed out a blast of steam as he adjusted his jacket to pull out his phone, whose screen was cracked. "I'll write the number down. Guess those protective cases aren't just a scam to get more money, huh?"

Sliver of Hope

Simon parked the jeep and couldn't help but notice his fuel gauge needle pointing at empty with the red light indicator next to it. He curled his lip at the smell of hot oil when he shut off the engine.

When he saw Tanya bent over, Simon ran back the length of the yard between them and stopped when he saw the other two people standing there with Blake. "Was she on the bike with you?"

Blake rubbed his head with a nod. "She had the helmet. Mo, do you mind giving Simon here an update?" He pointed at his phone. "This is the guy I was telling you about."

"Yeah, I can see why you guys ain't scared of nothin'," Mo said with wide eyes.

Mo and Simon walked away from the others toward the jeep as Mo cued up the video of the arson on Blush from earlier that night.

After the video played, Simon stared hard at Mo as his face pulled tight with anger. "And you just happened to be hiding out nearby, huh?" He grabbed Mo by his shirt and slammed him against the wall of the house hard, lifting him off his feet.

Mo was trying not to shout to keep any attention off them

as his face twisted with fear and he dropped his phone. "Hey man, chill! I had some beef with your brother, but it's cool now, okay? We're cool. I swear I had nothing to do with this!"

"What kind of beef? Do you know the fire starter?"

Mo explained as he tried to pull Simon's hands away. "No, dude! I don't know that asshole. I saw him and made the 9-1-1 call. That's it! Come on, man, before my sister sees you and starts screaming."

Simon let go of the young man and walked back to the others. He bent to check on Tanya and noticed Blake's cut pant leg. "Were you thrown?"

"Yeah," Blake answered. "The wreck wasn't bad. But any accident on a bike can be a nightmare. Our supper was interrupted. We should go grab a bite someplace and catch you up on things."

Simon helped Tanya to her feet, and when she saw his face she buried her own against his chest. He could hear her trying to say something but couldn't make sense of it.

"I think we better get going. Can I do anything to thank you for your help?" Simon asked the young woman in pink scrubs.

"Yes," the nurse replied. "Keep these two off of motorcycles. And if I see any of you again, it better be at the hospital and not in my kitchen in the middle of the night." She was smiling despite her serious tone. "Take care of these two.

Hey, and if you're looking for a place to eat at this hour, there's a place headed toward the hospital that's open twenty-four hours. The food is terrible, the service is worse, and the coffee tastes burnt, but it's always open, and it's pretty cheap."

Simon scooped Tanya up into his arms and gave the nurse a nod. "Enjoy your Thanksgiving. I appreciate what you two did for us."

"With my job, I'll be lucky to get a few bites of Turkey sandwich before the day is out," the nurse forced a laugh. "Don't go making my shift any busier, unless you're coming in to get an x-ray for your friend's leg."

"Gia, I told you, he don't like hospitals," Mo reminded her.

"Make up a name when you come in and ask for me," Gia said. "I can help push him in and out quickly."

Blake answered with a half-smile, "I couldn't do that. I might need the insurance to cover my bill."

"Fine," Gia said, crossing her arms. "But don't let it set like that for too long. Those little injuries can make you feel old before your time if not given good treatment. Now get out of here before my neighbors think I got two big white boyfriends fighting over me." She grinned at both men and went back inside her apartment with Mo.

Simon placed Tanya in the front seat and held the door for Blake. "Put that foot up on the seat and give it a rest. We gotta stop for gas, and then you two can figure out where you want to go over some coffee or something."

By the time they stopped to fill up, Tanya began to get restless in the uncomfortable seat. She began to flick through pictures on her cell phone when it rang in her hands. She nearly dropped it to the floor from the surprise but answered quickly when she saw Melissa's name.

"Missy?!" She almost yelled into the phone. "Where are you? Are you okay?" She sat upright and tucked her knee tight to her chest as if it would make a privacy wall between herself and the two men. "Don't start with me. You have no idea what I- No, I'm sorry. I just... I'll explain when I can… You're at a party?" She fought between emotions and tried to compose herself.

"No, I didn't go to work either. I was just, uh, sitting up working on a dress for this interview on Friday," she explained, wiping her wet cheeks. She reached out to stop Simon's hand when he settled back in to start the jeep and put a finger up to her lips. "I was hoping you'd go with me."

Tanya screwed up her face with confusion and gestured to no one. "No, I already talked to Mom and told her we can't make it home this week. But she's going to call us both when she sees the news. No, not the apartment. The club. There was a really bad fire. No! I never told them we work there, but it was awful, and I don't know who might have been in there or if they got out. But you know how Mom is. She'll start going on about crime and danger and beg us to come home."

Tanya got quiet as she listened. A few times, she took a breath like she might speak or cry. "Have you…have you heard from the other girls? No, I mean, I don't know if anyone-They might have just been shaken up and went home, but that was hours ago, so I thought maybe- No, I haven't either. Blake? No, I haven't seen him," she lied. "Do you think I should call him, or do you want to? Yeah, he sent me the same ad. That's the job thing tomorrow. Yeah, he sent me the same ad and said we should check it out."

"Yeah," she looked at Simon leaning back in the seat impatiently. "I gotta go too. Do you want to- Missy?" Tanya looked at the screen as it flashed CALL ENDED. She curled her fingers in frustration and bared her teeth as if she might scream. She took a breath to try to calm down when she noticed the men were watching her.

Simon turned the key and drove away from the pump just as a tanker parked at the wells.

"Did I hear right earlier?" Tanya asked as she looked back at Blake. "Did that guy send you the video?"

Blake nodded. Then he held up his broken cell phone. "I thought you didn't want to see it?"

"That was before I knew," Tanya said. "But after everything else today, I just- I feel like I need to know as much as I can. I want to go out there with you guys. Do what you do."

Blake curled up half a smile. "Says the girl who just lied to her sister about me. Why did you do that anyway?

176

"Because Simon told me she was bitten," she explained. "He also told me about your file and how you're trying to save your sister. If yours can be saved, maybe so can mine. I can't be with her until I know it can be done. And I won't go near her until I know how to defend myself in case…well, in case she can't."

Blake didn't answer right away. He stared at Simon in the rearview mirror long and hard, then set his jaw. Simon caught his gaze with intensity and lowered his eyes to hide his denial.

"So now you believe in vampires, huh? What else did he tell you?" Blake asked.

Simon kept his eyes on the road, avoiding both of his passengers. "Everything. She has a right. Nobody should be a helpless victim. And as you both ought to have learned from your little accident, I can't be everywhere. I can't protect you. Not from them. Not from myself."

"Oh, not this again," Blake groaned. "How long have we been doing this? And how many times are you gonna warn me about keeping my distance and being ready? As if there's anything I could do if I had to?"

"Wait," Tanya cut in. "You mean, you don't know how to deal with any of this?"

Blake shook his head with a hand up. "I didn't say that. I have dealt with some pretty hairy situations. But that doesn't mean I'm cocky enough to think I won't hesitate when it's my brother snarling in my face."

"Of the two of us, I trust you more than myself when it comes to hesitation," Simon said. "The only reason she's even out there is-"

"Oh, knock it off!" Blake cut him off. "We've been over this a hundred times. The only thing that might have gone differently in that subway is maybe I wouldn't have been bitten."

"What?! You were bitten too?" Tanya asked. "Are you a-"

"No, no, no." Blake stopped her. "I'm not saying I know how it all works, but I always make bank runs during the day. I eat food. I ain't one of them."

"Alright, well. So sunlight," Tanya changed her tone. "That's a real thing. It kills them. So that's why she never came home to stay. I believed her stupid doctor appointment excuse because I didn't know. Anyway, what else? Is it like the movies? You know, wooden stakes and holy water?"

"In theory," Simon chimed in. "Being honest with you, we've never gotten that close to finding out."

"Okay, so what about you then?" Tanya asked Simon without looking at him. "I mean, you know. What about your packmate who thinks I'm a vampire? How do I deal with him if he comes after me the next time you can't be around? I don't have a gun, so silver bullets are out. Not that I know how to shoot anyway."

Blake laughed. "Now that's a problem we can fix. Learning how to shoot is easy. The tough part is hitting a target that is actively threatening you. Not panicking. And right now, having access to a gun and ammo is a problem after what just happened. I lost everything but the sidearm I carry, with one magazine."

Simon made a turn and shook his head. "Of course, the catch to all that is, with what we're after now, guns are of little use. We mostly carry for human problems and mainly as a deterrent. Sure, a bullet can hurt me. But after everything I've been through, I couldn't tell you how many it might take. I always seem to get back up eventually. We have some normal flaws, like needing to breathe. So suffocation and drowning are possible. Decapitation is the most certain, but also the most risky." Simon gave a nod and finally stole a look at Tanya. "But silver does work. It's the reason Reno is missing a finger. That's how I knew who was in your apartment before I caught wind of him stowing in my jeep." Simon added, "Not that we can get much else we might need on a holiday, anyway. Not without ties to the mob or something."

Tanya turned her head just as Blake shot a quick look into the mirror. "So, what's your plan then?" Tanya asked. She threw her hands up in frustration. "Corner your target and tear them apart with your bare hands?"

Both men looked back at Tanya for a moment, then looked at each other seriously in the mirror.

Simon offered, "Well, you were okay with being bait yesterday. What's different now?"

Blake laughed at the comment. "Now she wants to be armed and learn to defend herself," he said to Simon. "If we come through this, maybe I'll even teach you how to fix my bike, Angel. In our kind of life, there's no such thing as having too many skills. You never know what might keep you alive. Even your costume-making could come in handy to get out of a pinch. Who knows?"

Simon turned the wheel again into a parking lot for the restaurant Gia suggested. He parked and looked at Tanya as he turned off the vehicle, "The plan was never about getting violent. We're trying to bring Leila home. If things have to get-"

"Hairy," Blake chimed in.

"If it gets complicated, it's helpful to be prepared for trouble," Simon finished.

Tanya looked around and noticed the parking lot was nearly half full. "You guys want to just get something to go instead of being around all these people for too long?"

Simon offered to go in and make an order, but Tanya plucked the prepaid card from her pocket before he could get out. She offered it to Simon. "Might as well put this to some use."

After Simon went inside, she watched as Blake fiddled with his broken phone. "So I can't help but notice you don't seem too upset about what happened."

Blake stared back and forced a fake half-smile. "It's just something I got used to. It's not going to serve any of us for me to get hell-bent and pissed off. Been in similar situations too many times. It's just been a while. The hardest part is not knowing. At least you got a phone call. With mine busted up, I have no way of knowing without going back there." He shrugged and let out a long breath as he shook his head. "But if I go back, it's going to be a trip down to the police station, and my statement and alibi, and none of it will look good for me. I'll probably go through booking, and they'll look at my priors and the recent insurance update. That I haven't taken a night off in a long time, and then as soon as I do…boom."

"I get it. Sorry I mentioned it." Tanya looked away.

"You have to. Somebody has to," Blake replied. "It's not going to just go away. It never does. I'm surprised it ever got as comfortable as it was. Easy, even." Blake's tone was more serious than she had ever heard. He had her full attention. "Once you've seen something, even as soon as you think you know something is out there that doesn't belong. Something that's after you or someone you care about. Or even just that shadows hold the same shape every time you see one, it starts to eat at you. Gets in your dreams. It knocks on your window when you try to sleep. It wakes you up in a sweat. It makes you make decisions you don't want to make."

"So, if you're okay talking about it, can you tell me about the file?" Tanya asked.

"I don't know what Simon told you," Blake began. "But, it was kind of my job to keep an eye out for anything that might lead us back to Leila. That's our sister. I clipped newspaper articles. I followed police cases. Sometimes I got more involved when I thought I might find who took her. She was bitten right under my nose in the club. But I didn't know that was what happened at the time. Until she attacked me."

"Right there in the club? Your sister was a stripper in your club? That's-"

"No, it wasn't like that. Not yet, anyway. She wanted to make that kind of money, but she was underage. She wanted a job, and she came looking for me," Blake went on. "I put her to work moving stuff around, cleaning the place after hours. Stocking the bar. The kind of stuff I did when I started there. I thought her old man would be pissed she was always coming home late, but she said he never paid her any attention. So it went on for a while, and she was a regular face the customers knew. Some guy took an interest in her and kept pushing her to get on stage. Then she kept pushing me to help her get a fake ID and make it happen."

Tanya let out a fake laugh. "What are big brothers for, right?"

"Hey, I barely knew her. We didn't grow up together. I was on my own for a while by the time she was even born. She brought me a picture of myself as a kid she stole from her mother's purse. My- Our mother. The way she talked about her old man kinda reminded me of my own, and I felt like I owed her something. So for her sixteenth birthday, I had the fake ID made up for her. I was gonna surprise her with it. But that guy who liked her had a different surprise for her.

I thought they were making out in a corner booth when we were closing. I kicked him out, and he took her with him. I felt like shit about it and followed them out. Chased his car to a subway to try to make sure she didn't do something stupid. I thought she was gonna run off with this guy and that I had pushed her to do it."

Blake rolled his neck and rubbed a scar under his stubble. Tanya took a good look at the ugly pink scar that, until he shaved for the reopening, had been hidden under his ginger beard hair.

Tanya asked, "What makes you think you can bring her home? You said she was turned. There isn't any way to… To undo that, is there?"

Simon returned with two takeout bags and handed them to Blake. "Hope you guys figured out where we're going."

Patching Things Up

Simon slept with his wide-brimmed fedora over his face in a chair facing the hotel door. Tanya was in one of the double beds alone with the covers drawn over her head and had fallen asleep almost as soon as she crawled into it.

Blake had been unable to sleep since removing his boots when his ankle swelled almost immediately with pain and stiffness. He resigned himself to laying back on the bed with his leg propped up on some spare pillows with a towel full of ice. He occupied his time trying to dismantle his phone with his pocket knife to see if he could get it working again.

The only result of his work was some green and blue light on the screen that scribbled across the larger pieces of the unbroken glass for a moment just when he pulled the seams apart. Blake tossed his now useless pieces of the phone on the bed next to himself and searched for the television remote when he saw Tanya's phone lying next to her on the other bed. He struggled to get up and limped on his bad ankle over to pick up her phone, but it didn't take long to decide it was useless without her password.

Blake saw Simon shift and recross his legs but didn't seem to wake. Blake hobbled over to where their coats hung near the door and searched the pockets for his flip phone. When he found it, he went to the door to walk outside and Simon sat upright.

"What's going on? Someone out there?" Simon asked.

Blake spoke softly back with his empty hand up. "No, I'm just going to get some more ice and see if the vending machines have anything to keep me awake and maybe some pain pills. You need anything?"

Simon shook his head, replaced his hat, and settled back into a slouch.

Blake closed the door quietly and limped to the vending and laundry area down the hall. He reached into his pocket for the phone and flipped it open to dial a number. The time on the screen read just before six o'clock.

"Hey, it's me," Blake spoke with a low voice as he checked the hallway. "I had to borrow a phone. Mine was broken. Just checking in to make sure things are still on for tomorrow. Yeah, she mentioned getting dolled up to be there, so even with everything going on here, I'm sure she'll still be there. Nothing I can't handle. Just some setbacks with the business. No, if anything it should give her the push she needs to move on."

Blake swiped his card at each of the two vending machines and gathered up a couple of candy bars and a bottled soda. "I remember you said you want both. They do everything together. Nothing to worry about. Yeah, we'll talk after."

Blake rifled through the settings to delete the dialed number and accidentally erased every recent call. "Dammit! Too late now."

He made his way unevenly back to their door and scanned the card for entry. Tanya had turned over and rolled herself up snugly in the layers of blankets with her head still covered. Blake shut the door as gently as possible and replaced the phone inside Simon's coat pocket.

Blake crawled back up onto the bed and wrapped his foot into the towel where most of the ice had melted.

"Time to wake up," Simon announced. "Maid service is on its way, and if we're still here in fifteen minutes they'll charge another night we don't need."

Simon gathered the remaining food leftovers at the door and helped Blake to his feet. "I don't recommend putting that boot back on. I'll walk you out so you can keep weight off of it. Do you want to go to the hospital?"

"You think it would look better for the inevitable police report later if I have a doctor's note?" Blake joked.

"We don't really have anywhere else to be right now, and you could use a cast on that foot," Simon suggested.

"Alright, alright. I don't see much of a choice," Blake said as he leaned on Simon. "Just like old times, huh?"

"Yeah," Simon added sarcastically. "Getting you patched up is the second job I never wanted."

Simon helped Blake settle into the jeep's backseat and drove back to pick up Tanya with the bags at the door. "I think once we get checked in, I'm gonna call Phie and see if she has any update. We still have a lot on our plate."

"Phie?" Blake perked up. "Haven't heard that name in a while. Does that mean I finally get to meet-"

"Cool it, will ya?" Simon cut him off. "She's off limits for you. Don't need you using your injury for her sympathy. But it's probably the best place to lay low under supervision so you can heal right now. You ran your credit card to book the hotel room, so if police are looking for you, they're gonna catch up fast if we stay in the city too long."

Simon drove them to the hospital and started the check-in process before returning to the waiting room with Blake and Tanya. "I'll go make the call to Phie, and I think I better go take care of some business of my own for an hour or two. Should be enough time to get you set with what you need here?"

Tanya looked back at Simon. "You're just going to leave us here?"

Simon bent close to Tanya. "I shouldn't be around a lot of people for a long period of time. In places like this, it's difficult to judge my ability to control my, uh, temper. This is not the place I want to be if the urge starts to creep up on me." He stood up and adjusted his coat. "Call me when you're ready if I'm not back by then. I won't go too far."

"I could go with you. You could tell me more about how all that works," she offered.

"If I feel it's not safe for them, it's not safe for you either," Simon said. "Besides, I need to make that call, and someone needs to keep Blake from walking out before he gets treated."

Simon gave them his best assuring smile and turned to leave.

Tanya watched the doors to the emergency room and glanced back toward the front windows from time to time for Simon's jeep every few minutes since he left. The receptionist had already called back the only other people waiting and she couldn't help but check the time every so often.

"So, were you still thinking about that job offer?" Blake asked as he ate the last bit of candy bar from the hotel.

"What?" Tanya asked off-guard. "I mean, it's on my mind some, I guess. Tomorrow feels pretty far away with everything else right now."

"Today will fly by before you know it," Blake said. "You might keep your mind busy hunting down something to wear since your closet is out of reach."

"That's not a terrible idea," Tanya answered. "Anything's better than all this quiet. You think your new girlfriend is working today?"

Blake looked back toward the ER doors and made a disappointed face. "I hope so. Gia said she could help speed things up if I came in."

"How do you do that? Keep all the names straight, I mean. Yet you only ever call me Angel?" Tanya asked.

"Well, that's the name I've been calling you for since you started working for me," Blake explained. "It's easier to not flip-flop with names to keep them all straight. Speaking of which, is there a way to call my phone and check for messages?"

"Yeah, no problem. I should have thought of that last night," she replied.

"Mr. Gentry, you can come back now," a familiar voice called out. Gia stood in the doorway to the emergency room with a clipboard.

"Speak of the devil," Tanya said. "We can check your calls once we get settled in."

Simon's phone rang while he was waiting in traffic at a light not far away from the hospital. He tightened his grip on the steering wheel and clenched his teeth while he looked for an opening to pull over.

Once he was off the road, he pulled out his flip phone and checked the call. When he saw only one call listed in the history, he flipped through his settings to see if there was a message indicating a reset or other problems. He clicked send on the number for Phie from her missed call.

"Hey- I know I should just check the message first, but I don't have company," Simon said into the phone. "Well, yeah. I did come in to pick up my brother. He's in the hospital right now. No, he's fine. Just a sprain, we hope, but he's getting an X-ray to make sure."

Simon checked his rearview mirror to watch a police cruiser approaching and made sure it passed before continuing. "Dinner? What about Reno? I really should keep an eye on these two. Yeah, Angel is sitting with him. They work together. I don't know if they- No, it's not important to me. What would I care if-?" Simon sighed into the phone and couldn't help but laugh.

"Tell you what? I'll invite them, and you can play matchmaker if you want, okay?" Simon suggested. "How could I say no to your cooking? Alright, I'll see you in a few hours."

Simon ended the call and, for a moment, looked over at the empty seat beside himself. When he heard a horn blast from a big rig hauling an oversized load, he snapped back to attention and merged back into traffic quickly.

Mama's Table

Hours passed with Tanya pacing the waiting room while it filled slowly with other patients. She called Simon to return just as Blake was handling his discharge forms. When Gia escorted Blake out in his new boot splint and a pair of crutches, Tanya had to rush him to finish his goodbyes so they could finally leave the hospital.

"Well, at least we're finally getting out of this place," Tanya said with a sigh of relief. "I never did like hospitals. Do we have some kind of plan for the rest of the day?"

Simon turned the key in the jeep and answered, "We've been invited to Thanksgiving dinner at just about the only place we have left to go we don't have to pay for."

"Something to eat sounds good after watching your brother try to put moves on his new favorite nurse," Tanya said as she gestured at Blake, who was grinning shamelessly. "My stomach has been lurching all afternoon."

"He's probably not used to having that effect on a woman," Simon said. "I suppose that makes you special in a way."

"Nah," Blake interrupted. "They all see something in me eventually."

"So far, you've at least been a pain in my neck," Tanya joked. "I can say that now that you're not my boss, right?"

Blake shot her a look and looked like he might explode for a moment. "I guess I deserved that. I know I said we could talk, but do you mind watching the cheap shots?"

"Sorry," Tanya apologized and turned her face away. "It's still raw for me too. I have too much time to think about things and it's just souring, you know?" She took a heavy breath and turned herself in the seat to look at Blake more directly. "You made the schedule, right? So you know who was supposed to be there last night?"

"Yeah, I do. And if I was sure I wouldn't be in cuffs right now, I'd go back and see what I can find out," Blake answered. "It looks bad, you know that, right? I get called out last minute, my bike is wrecked not even a block away. The ink on the new papers for the place was barely even dry. And the most recent big expense on the books, if investigated, went to you, who happens to be with me right now, still avoiding the police. I tried to tell you. I just have to push through it for now."

Tanya nodded and pulled her knee up to her chest. "I just think I'm some kind of bitch for not being more upset about it. Like, one minute I'm sick in a stranger's flower beds, and the next I'm just back to, 'Okay, T, you still need a new apartment, and you're out of clean clothes, and Missy's okay even if she's not right here with you.'" She reached up to pull her hair back and scratched at the diminished scar underneath. "Why am I like this? I feel like I should care more."

Simon looked over while they were at a traffic light. "You

probably don't want to hear it, but most likely just getting through that initial shock is what makes you feel okay. A lot has happened to you in a short time. And this time it wasn't you."

Blake nodded in agreement. "This morning was the first restful sleep you've had in a while. Am I right? And even though we spent most of the day at the hospital, you weren't checking your phone every three seconds for good news? You know things aren't okay, but right now is okay enough to move forward." His mouth pulled to one corner, and he shrugged. "Or, in my case, you'd be surprised by the kinds of things you can handle when you know that being an emotional wreck only makes things worse."

"I do worry about them, you know?" Tanya asked after a short awkward silence. "But somehow, even though I was right there with them a week ago doing the job, making jokes together, bragging about tips, or complaining about life together… It's just… It's weird. Like they were a movie I watched that you get upset about for a minute, and then the movie is over, and I don't need to watch it again."

Both men nodded but didn't answer. Tanya turned back to face forward and looked out from the bridge they were crossing. "It's just crazy how no matter what happens or who it affects, the rest of the world just keeps moving on like it didn't make any difference."

After the droning hum of the grated bridge, Simon soon turned off the main highway on the gravelly dirt roads into the woods. The unpaved road into the woods was rutted and bumpy. Especially with the recent downpour that created deep grooves going every which direction as Simon navigated the climb further between sprawls of dense, leafless trees.

Blake took his time clambering out of the jeep once they had parked at what looked like a crumbling group of cabins used as a summer camp some time ago. Dormitory buildings with torn screens and damaged roofs, and missing doors stood in rows on either side of a larger main building whose broad, raised porch jutted out toward a wide fire pit circle that still had a few logs arranged where campers may sit around at night and tell stories while they roasted treats.

He could smell the breeze blowing in, carrying over dead leaves that littered most of the grounds in sight. Blake took his time following the other two up to the main building, careful not to catch his crutches on hidden obstacles that might trip him.

Once inside, Simon quickly made introductions to a short black woman with bright amber eyes he called Mama.

"I bet that name got some attention growing up, huh?" Blake joked to the new acquaintance.

"Find another name to call me, boy, and I'll tan your hide 'til you get it right," Mama answered. "Come on in and sit down a minute."

Blake raised his brow and nodded smugly. "You should have

prepared me better, Simon. You know I like a girl with some moxy."

Tanya shot him a look he could barely see in his peripheral, and she rolled her eyes before she turned to look around the place.

"That ain't all you'll get if you sass Mama in her own house." Mama approached him and took his crutches when he sat on the pew seat opposite the wood stove kitchen area. She stored them under the seat and took hold of Blake's leg above the splinted ankle to prop it on the bench while he turned in place to accommodate her dauntless insistence. Then she helped Blake remove his leather jacket to fold it over as a makeshift pillow and tucked it behind his shoulder to cushion against the hard wooden edge of the pew.

"Just when I thought I'd seen all the nurses I could handle for one day," Blake laughed.

"Oh Child! Mama plays nurse, cook, teacher, maid, laundress, and just about anything else for her boys." Mama crossed her arms as she cast a look toward Simon. "At least until they think they grown and see fit to replace me."

Simon took off his coat and hat to hang them near the door and made himself sound serious. "Why would we ever do something like that? Nobody could hope to fill your shoes."

"Don't you start on me now," Mama said on her way back to the stove. "You know I got no time for them buttermilk biscuit lies of yours. They go straight to my hips."

Blake watched her every move, mostly from the waist down, as she walked away and stood facing the stove. Simon obstructed his view by bringing mess kit dishes to the pool table and began to set places between each of the pockets for six.

Tanya grabbed what she could of the odd pieces Simon left in the kitchen to help him set the table while Mama switched one pot from the stove and began stirring in another. "Do you mind if we set one more place in case Mi- In case Rose calls me back?"

Simon paused and looked up at Blake without answering.

"Who's that, Angel?" Mama asked with interest.

"She's my sister." Tanya tucked her hair behind her ear and looked at Blake. "She probably made other plans, but-"

"Oh, baby," Mama cut her off. "If she's family of yours, there's room at Mama's table. The boys'll be coming in a minute. Can already smell the wet of the lake on 'em comin' up."

Blake watched Mama whisk herself around the kitchen as Simon and Tanya finished moving benches to the table and filling cups with water at each place setting. He had to shift in the pew to prop up his other foot and winced when he tried to cross them over each other.

He had finally begun to look around the room and noticed several parts of the balcony railing above and part of the rafters in need of repair. Old nails jutted out of the log wall where something heavy may have hung over the back door, and an out-of-place portable television Mama removed from the buffet table made him grin. Blake watched her again as she took it out of the room until the scraping of the back door digging into the floor caught his attention.

He began to reach down for his crutches as two men came in, chattering over each other. They carried a set of shoes and clothes and wore only pants. Their hair was dripping, and their pants showed wet spots any place their bodies bent to wrinkle. The chilly draft that swept into the room with the men made the hair stand up on Blake's arms even after the door was slammed closed.

"Y'all come just in time," Mama greeted. "Put on a shirt or somethin' now. We got company for supper. Everything is as hot as I could keep it. So sit yourselves down and behave so we can pray."

Blake made his way to the table, to a place next to Tanya, across from Simon but hadn't sat down yet. The shorter and fitter of the two men sat at the head of the table facing the front door, while the taller of the two sat next to Simon and pulled his sandy hair into a ponytail with a band from his wrist.

"Before I get too comfy again, can you point me to the can?" Blake asked.

Simon pointed to the back door. "Right outside, chained to the tree. It gets windy up here."

"No place to wash before we eat?" he asked again.

"There's still some clean water in the pitcher, baby," Mama nodded to the buffet table where she was placing pots to serve each of the dishes with stew. "There's some dish soap in the cabinet under the counter. Use a bowl if you need, and I'll toss it out for you after supper. See that, boys? We have a gentleman in the house who washes up without being told."

"I bet he sits down to piss," the man at the head of the table quipped.

"What did you say at Mama's table?" Mama scolded. "Mr. Joshua, that mouth of yours can go hungry tonight if you wanna keep a filthy tongue."

Blake saw a look of challenge on the face of Mr. Joshua, who glared at him. The man shot a look at Mama like he might double down to see if she'd back up her threat. Blake crutched his way back to the pew against the wall without bothering with the water pitcher and fumbled with his jacket to put it back on.

"No need to wait on the prayer, Mama," Blake suggested. "I haven't had practice hobbling around on crutches in a dark shed before, and the draft your boys let in will have your food cold by the time I figure it out."

"What's the problem?" Mr. Joshua asked. "Cold got you tucked up inside?"

Blake ignored the comment and started toward the back door when Mama raised her voice. "Now I done told you behave yourself! Both of you. Or so help me I'll strap you together in the closet 'til you can get along. I will not have my Thanksgiving spoiled by this kind of talk. You better not try me. I've been working all day on this stew. And you," she pointed at Blake. "Bow your head while we pray, and then you may be excused. We all plenty hungry, and I've had about enough, you hear?"

Blake surveyed the room with all eyes fixed uncomfortably on him except for Mr. Joshua. He bowed his head and made himself steady on his crutches to wait.

"Fisher, baby," Mama started. "It's a new moon for you. Would you kindly lead us in prayer with thanks tonight?"

Fisher nodded and folded his hands. "May we all-"

The back door crashed open behind Blake, and a large man, out of breath carrying a teenage ginger-haired girl, burst into the room, which caused Tanya to jump and scream.

The man was almost panting as he tried to get his words out. "Mama, they're coming for her! I didn't know where else to go. They're coming fast!"

The room stood, with Mr. Joshua putting himself between the back door and the others at the table. Mr. Joshua growled at the man and squared himself as if to attack him.

Mama rushed over between the men and took the girl into her arms. She looked back at the others at the table fearfully and carefully transferred the young girl over to Mr. Joshua. "Take her and those two and get outta here, now. We'll run them off as best we can."

"Phie, I can't just-"

Mama slapped Mr. Joshua hard across the face. "I done told y'all plenty that I don't hear that name in my house! Go now, I said!"

Simon almost leaped across the room to help Blake through the front door with Tanya close behind them. "Tanya, get the key out of my coat pocket. Drive them as far away from here as you can get!"

Blake was barely in the passenger seat when he heard a group of howls pierce the still night air. Tanya cranked the ignition as Mr. Joshua climbed into the back seat with the girl and shouted at Tanya to drive. Simon slammed Blake's door closed, and his clothing melded into his body to be replaced by coarse hair before he turned to run into the woods.

Power Shift

Tanya ground the reverse gear in her hurry, and the jeep lurched and stalled. She twisted the key again and screamed at the wheel as she spun it with the accelerator floored until they were pointed away from the cabin and corrected with a hard bump as she drove over a dead log near the fire pit.

Blake shouted at her to shift as the engine groaned and they spun into the dark. "Headlights! Come on, Angel, you got this!"

Tanya swerved away from a tree just as the lights came on, and she slid off the dirt road into a rut that nearly made them tip over. The path to the road was barely visible through the dingy windshield and how dark the night in the woods had become.

"You're gonna kill us!" Joshua said. "Can you drive?"

Blake pulled a pistol from under his jacket and pointed it at Joshua. "SHUT the FUCK up! She's doing just fine. Ain't that right, Angel?"

Tanya blinked away impending tears and nodded at the windshield. "Enough. I'm okay enough. I got this."

Tanya grabbed the shifter and missed a gear but slammed it into the next without letting off the gas pedal, with the jeep bumping down the path and swerving to get in the road.

"Well, that's power-shifting down," Blake grinned as he looked out the window. "Use the clutch when you grab the next one. You're doing fine. Smaller corrections on the wheel now. There you go, level it out and take the last gear. That's it."

"Are you serious?" Joshua yelled. "This is when you want to teach driver's ed?"

Blake clicked the hammer back and refused to look at Joshua. "Brake early on the turns, then jam the gas to get out again."

Tanya slid through most of a gentle curve and put her foot down as the jeep resisted. She could hear something like snarling or growling close by but resisted looking anywhere but the narrow dirt road until she had straightened out the vehicle.

"Right, I forgot downshifting," Blake apologized. "My fault. Just press the clutch and take it back to third now. That's up in the middle. Okay, upshift again to fourth which is straight down. We're fine."

Joshua sounded panicked. "She's starting to turn!"

Tanya saw Blake looking back and he almost spoke. She glanced into the rearview mirror to see Joshua wrestling with the teenage girl in his arms. "What are you doing?"

Blake chided, "Eyes on the road, Angel. Your job is saving us, remember?"

"She's changing, man," Joshua said. "I got to get her out of here."

Howling could be heard behind them again just before Tanya felt the cold wind coming through the interior. In the rearview mirror, she could see Joshua reaching up through the soft top with a hairy arm and tearing away a section of the overhead, leaving a large flap whipping about as it clung to the seam. Joshua growled loudly and jumped up from the seat out of the jeep into the cloud of dust behind them. When she looked into the side mirror, she could see yellow eyes coming closer and then suddenly change direction once Joshua and the girl were gone.

"What now?" Tanya asked.

Blake turned forward and shouted, "Slow down! That's the main road coming up. You'll throw us on the bump!"

Tanya downshifted and eased into the brake, but the bump from the dirt road to the blacktop still hit hard enough to bounce her in her seat, and the tail end pounded onto the pavement. She held the wheel with white knuckles on one hand and geared up with the other as the tires squealed to catch a grip.

"Okay, now that was sexy," Blake said. He finally uncocked and reholstered his gun.

Tanya kept up speed until they reached the intersection before the bridge. "Don't get your hopes up. I wouldn't sleep with a guy wearing a cast. I might hurt you," she joked.

"Might just be my lucky day then. This is just a splint," Blake reminded her. "I don't get fitted for a cast until the swelling goes down."

"Do you think they're gone? I feel like we abandoned them," Tanya said.

Blake shook his head. "We did what we had to do. We gave them a chance to defend themselves. And you got us down here so we could live to fight another day. Even if we were prepared for a fight like that, we wouldn't have had much chance on the mountain in the woods like that. Especially at night."

"So we'll check in with Simon once we get further out." Tanya spun through a stop sign and turned toward the bridge before daring to look behind them in the mirror again. "Where are we going anyway?"

"As much as I hate to say it, I should go look at the damage to Blush," Blake admitted. "But that'll have to be done once other places start opening so I can replace this broken phone and pull what strings I still have to avoid a trip downtown. For now, it's looking like another hotel. As far away from here as this thing can still take us after the beating it just took."

Tanya stole a look over at him and tried to joke. "You sound like you're gonna call up your mob friends to put a hit out on the fire marshal before he makes any case on the place or something."

Blake didn't answer right away. She couldn't see any change in his expression in the dark when she looked over at him. "You watch too much TV," he said, finally.

"Can I ask you why you took up for me back there?" Tanya asked, finally driving at a reasonable speed as they approached traffic.

"Well," Blake answered. "If we were going to crash or get caught by werewolves, I'd much rather it have been because you did your best and it didn't work out. He was only making things worse. There was nothing that idiot could do to help except shut his yapper."

Tanya smiled with pursed lips. "You just- Nevermind."

"I just what?"

"You reminded me of my dad," she said. "He always has my back. And it took a lot of pressure off. Like you believed in me the way he always does. I really miss him."

Blake was silent until the droning of the bridge grates was behind them. "You can just go home, you know?"

"No. I can't." Tanya stretched her arms and twisted her grip tightly on the steering wheel. "Not without Missy."

"If you're waiting for her, don't," Blake said too easily. "After you get the new job, go home and celebrate with your folks. Whether she can go with you or not. You'll wind up just like us if you don't live your own life."

"I thought you said this was how life is for you guys now?" Tanya asked.

Blake laughed. "Sure it is, now. Simon is a special case, but he still could have tried to go home. Now he thinks he can't unless he can bring Leila home with him. To prove he's not too dangerous to at least visit from time to time. And I let myself get sucked into this life, but that was years after I had already sabotaged myself. Now I know I could go back. I just haven't decided if I want to. It's not like she ever came looking for me."

"She who? Your mother?"

"Forget it," Blake said. "It's not important."

"That's not how that works," she looked at him as she brought the jeep to a stop at a red light. "We're kind of a team now, right? Are you gonna give up on me someday just because you think she quit on you?"

"I said forget it! Just drive."

Tanya pumped the clutch to shift, and the engine stalled. She tried the key, but the engine wouldn't turn over.

"Alright, just give it a minute," Blake said.

The smell of burning oil and black smoke billowed out from the hood.

"Well, isn't that just icing on the cake?" Tanya asked

sarcastically as she looked up through the hole torn in the top. "All we need now is some rain."

"Rain might do us some good in case we're still being followed," Blake added.

"I really didn't need to hear that." Tanya moved the stick shift to neutral and got out to push. "Steer it off the road. We may have bad luck, but we don't need any attention from stopped traffic." She pushed from behind and found it moved easily on the flat city street.

Once the jeep was off the road, Blake pulled the parking brake and joined Tanya on the shoulder. "I guess I dropped my crutches in all the hurry. Mind if I lean on you so we can keep moving?"

"Yeah, fine." Tanya reached into the jeep to untangle her purse from between the seats and hunkered under Blake's arm to start walking into the city. "As soon as we make some space between us and the breakdown, I'm gonna call a cab. Hopefully, it's late enough we won't have to wait long. We'll need to give them a destination. Which hotel are we going to?"

Blake leaned on her as easily as he could and stepped tenderly with the splint as much as possible. "There's an electronic place a few blocks over next to a cheap motel. Two birds with one stone. I think there's also a bus stop right around the corner where we can sit to wait on a ride. Are you calling a legit company or one of those gig drivers?"

"Whichever is cheaper, I guess," she answered. "At least it feels a little warmer walking than with that wind coming through the roof."

Tanya felt a sprinkle of rain in her hair just before they reached the bus stop.

Melissa sat in her room, styling her hair into layered curls. She had already scribbled a note for Thaddeus to thank him for his advice and the gift of hair care items and makeup kit he had waiting for her when she woke. She could hear a door slam on the upper floor when she lay down the curling iron and unplugged it. When she went to the hallway to investigate the sound, she could see Thaddeus in his driver's coat escorting Atticus out the front door.

She made her way back up the hall to Dusty's door but got no answer when she knocked. Melissa opened it to peek inside but saw no one there. Dusty's room was decorated with framed posters, playbills, and pairs of drama masks. The square king bed had a heavy red velour curtain like you might see on a stage that was drawn apart with gold ropes.

Melissa closed the door and knocked across the hall where she hoped to find Kitty might answer, but none came. She returned to her room and unlocked her phone to call Dusty's number. There was no ring tone and went straight to voicemail. She didn't leave a message.

She used her phone to find the local news and typed in FIRE.

The search produced several articles and feeds of videos that had been uploaded within the last day that proved Tanya's scare about the Blush club was genuine. She watched the first few seconds of one stream of firefighters on the scene with a crowd gathered around. The article she opened first showed a picture of the ruins of the building, charred and toppled in on itself.

Melissa made her way to the main hall while staring at Tanya's number on the screen of her phone. She opened her messages and saw no new replies from any recent conversations. She called Blake's number, but it also skipped to voicemail.

Melissa searched for any information on Shadow Puppets and saw that it would be open despite the holiday with an offer for a reduced price cover charge. The page showed the same advertisement Blake had sent her, with the added stamp over it that read SOLD OUT.

She found a number to call for a taxi and requested one to pick her up outside a nearby bar in an hour. When she realized the walk would consume more than half of that time while walking in heels, she added some pep to her step. The world around her blurred by until she was a few steps from the door to the upscale establishment she intended. Two men in suits that were outside smoking thin cigars looked surprised to see her suddenly on the well-lit street and argued politely over which would open the door for her. Once it was decided, she thanked them with a plastic smile and entered with her heels clicking on the polished hardwood floor.

Inside the main lounge, she could see there were only a few tables occupied by older couples, and at the bar, only four stools were occupied by men. Each of the patrons was well-dressed and much older than herself by at least a decade. She chose a seat at the bar at the corner so she could be seen by anyone but still avoided the mirrored glass behind the alcohol bottles racked behind the bar. The decor was simple, with dim track lighting and photos of nighttime cityscapes from around the world.

An older man who wore a silver cravat with a dark blue blazer sipped something clear from a short-stemmed balloon glass. He noticed her right away and watched boldly without looking away as Melissa climbed carefully onto the stool and waited for the bartender. When she ordered a cranberry martini, the man watching her immediately offered to pay for it and asked if he could join her.

"A lady shouldn't be drinking alone on a holiday," he began with a look of concern. "But if you'll accept the company of an old codger, neither of us have to sit alone. I'm Hank." He drank with his left hand with swollen veins as if he were showing off his tarnished gold wedding band.

The bartender was a woman in her thirties, with tired circles under her eyes that were lightly masked by concealer makeup. She had her springy blonde curls pulled up high and introduced herself as Del. When she approached, she slid a coaster under Hank's glass before he set it down. She turned to start mixing Melissa's drink in a long-stemmed traditional V-shaped martini glass.

Melissa gave Hank a nod in greeting and pointed at Hank's ring. "Where's your wife, Hank? Won't she worry you're not home to tuck her in?"

"If that's what you're sure you want to talk about, she's probably parked on her fat ass in curlers watching game show reruns halfway through her second bottle of Moscato," Hank grinned. "I'd rather talk about you. What the hell is a young wildcat doing in a place like this?"

When Del delivered her drink, Melissa reached for her glass, but Hank took her hand before she could reach it.

"You're freezing cold, dolly," he said. "You're certainly not dressed for the weather."

Melissa looked hard at his hand and eased her grip back into his with welcome. "This place should warm me up just fine, Hank. But if it doesn't, I'm sure you could help me with that problem."

"Well, aren't you a fireball?" Hank's row of white eyebrows raised high under a thick, perfectly styled side-part toupee. "You got a fancy for older men or something?"

Melissa finally locked eyes with him and said, "I'll be up-front with you. When I see power in a man, my legs can't manage to stay together. I can see by the way you handle yourself that you take what you want. And if you treat me real nice, I'll happily return the favor."

Hank reached into his jacket and produced a long wallet. He

put a gold-colored credit card on the table and slid it toward the leather interior cushion. "If it's power you like, I've owned and sold more businesses than I can even recall the names of. I started investing when I was still running a paper route and mowing lawns in the old neighborhood. I bought stock in the kind of technologies pretty young things like you use every day as commonplace and take for granted. Sunk everything I had into evolving computers used anywhere from traffic lights to the space program before I even had any bills of my own."

"I have to admit there's something special about a man who knows what a girl wants to hear." Melissa traced her fingers across Hank's wristwatch and turned in her stool in a way that made her dress creep up her thighs. "I have to use the ladies' room for a moment. If I'm not back in two minutes, you can be sure it's because you've had an effect on me." She winked at him and walked back into the corner to the restrooms.

Once inside, she made herself visible in the mirror. She sat on the sink counter to remove her black thong panties and hike up her skirt to expose herself openly with spread legs. Hank did not disappoint her and appeared in the doorway just as she was positioned as she liked.

She held a finger to her lips and then curled it toward her to summon him closer. As soon as he was within reach, she extended her bare legs to wrap around him and pull him closer. Hank was breathing heavily as she reached down to open the zipper fly of his slacks, and he leaned close to try to kiss her. She put a finger up between their mouths.

"I never kiss on the lips, Hank. Seems a silly rule. But I find it much more intimate than other things." Melissa smiled broadly and removed her finger to lean into his chest more closely. She leaned her chin on his shoulder and whispered. "I hope you don't mind the rules of a silly girl."

He chuckled and began to speak when she sank her fangs into his neck. She drank deeply, tasting the gin in his blood go straight to her head like guzzling from the bottle.

He appeared dizzy and weak when she loosed her grip on him and licked the wound closed. His mouth had dropped open, and his eyes were closed wide with pleasure as he attempted to steady himself. She reached into his jacket for his wallet, removed the cash she found there, and placed his wallet on top of her lacy underwear.

"Mmm! I hope you enjoyed that, Hank." Melissa stood on unsure legs and basked in the blurry buzz of liquor coursing through her blood. "You were exactly what I needed tonight. Maybe I'll see you again."

She walked out of the restroom while smoothing her plain cocktail dress and pushed the roll of cash deep into her cleavage.

When Del saw her come out alone, she asked if Melissa was okay.

"Oh, don't worry about me," Melissa winked. "But Hank is going to want to take a cab home tonight. Too much gin thins the blood."

One Life for Another

Simon shook off the disorientation and the pungent smell of someone else's blood and bile while hunched over the face-down body of an unfamiliar young man. Simon had undoubtedly taken his life. The man's body was twisted with blood pooling into the dirt and leaves. Fisher came to his side out of breath and turned over the corpse away from Simon.

Fisher shook his head with a relieved tone. "He's gutted. Better him than us, right?"

"Today, maybe." Simon stood and smelled the air. "No matter how many times we justify killing, it's still killing. He looks even younger than you. Just a kid."

Fisher nodded seriously when their eyes met. "Yeah, I know. Don't say it. Let's find the others."

Simon and Fisher followed tracks, and the breeze blew a familiar scent that made Simon start running deeper into the trees. He took on the form of a four-pawed wolf to cover ground more quickly without the distraction of colors or having to duck his head under low branches. His heightened senses caught the sound of Fisher close behind, following his lead, and he soon heard another set of paws join from the side that he recognized as Reno by size and scent.

The three of them slowed and stood into human form when they found Mama. She sat in the dirt, rocking her body gently while singing a lullaby. She held the teen girl close in a meld of shadows in the dark.

"Sweet water, pass by, on a bed of sleeping starlight.
Babble on, til the sun dares to shine.
Roll away, now, and go on, til you find your tomorrow.
Sweet baby flow now, on you go.
Never the same as yesterday."

Reno gave Simon a nudge and nodded toward a thick tree that lay over nearby. When Simon followed the gesture, his eyes landed on a slumped body impaled on the jagged remains of a broken branch that jutted upward. Simon leaped over the log to take hold of Joshua and remove him when Mama cried out just above a whisper.

"Don't you touch my baby!" Mama warned. "He needs his sleep now." Mama stroked the hair of the young girl in her lap, who was trembling but quiet. "Don't you worry none. Hush now. Mama's gonna sing you to sleep."

Joshua's head lay back with his eyes wide open toward the sky. His throat was torn away by large teeth down to sinew. At his feet, Simon could see a trail of blood and a parting of leaves where a body had been dragged away.

Melissa tipped the driver and exited the cab near the entrance to Shadow Puppets. She cut to the front of the line of people at the door and introduced herself to the doorman. At the sound of complaints from the queue, she turned and hissed at them and bared her sharp teeth. She was met with bored applause and some laughter in return. One of the girls in front of the line made a threatening gesture with her long fingernails and then laughed out loud.

"Cleo sent me an invite to come see about a job." Melissa reached into her purse for her phone and showed the message from Blake to the doorman as if she was showing a receipt at will-call.

The doorman stood towering over her with a broad chest and ignored her phone screen as he ushered in a group of teenagers. Behind his sunglasses, she couldn't see if he looked in her direction at all.

"Hey, I said I'm supposed to be here to meet your boss," Melissa said more insistently as she tried to stare into his eyes to assert herself.

When she was given no attention from him a second time, she tried to walk in with a group and was met by the doorman placing his arm between her and the entryway.

"You'll go if and when I say you can go," he said. "Not before."

Melissa adjusted herself and fixed a glare at the doorman. "Is there some sort of problem?"

"Customers first," he said without turning his head toward her.

The line wasn't very long, but Melissa counted to herself across busy lips the lights on that faced the street from a nearby building, the beats that thumped from the music inside, the cars as opposed to trucks as opposed to service vehicles that passed by, and of course the people going through to the club until she was the last one standing outside.

The doorman uncrossed his arms and flicked his thumb across a cell phone screen and a few more minutes passed before the screen changed in the reflection on his dark glasses as she watched.

"I'll escort you to Lady Cleo," he said. "Follow me."

He hooked a red rope behind them as they entered a dark tunnel of drop cloth that was pricked throughout with a vine of twinkling lights. At the end of the dim entry, the music was too loud to hear words from any of the moving mouths on the main floor. Some dancers stepped in beat to moving lights on the floor, others huddled near the bar, and as with most clubs of its kind, there was already a short line waiting outside the ladies' room. Melissa followed toward a set of stairs leading upward behind a back curtain that blended in with the lack of decor behind the bar area. Another security man with slicked hair held the curtain while they passed through.

The staircase twisted around at each landing that led to other closed doors until they reached the third floor. It was here that the doorman pressed a buzzer and turned to leave.

"I trust you can introduce yourself," he said. "Enjoy your evening."

By the time the doorman left her sight, the buzzer clicked loudly to release its lock. Melissa pushed inward to find a young, black-haired woman who sat at an elaborate switchboard and watched the club through a row of downward-slanted windows. Her hair was tied back in a simple ponytail, and she wore a plain, long-sleeved black outfit typical of a backstage worker of a theater production.

"You're early," the woman said. "Close the door and sit down with me a minute while I cue up the next sequence."

Melissa took the empty chair next to the woman and spun it into position. Her eyes darted over the panel of blinking lights, sliders, buttons, and knobs.

Melissa said, "I guess you're pretty busy this time of night, huh?"

"No, I mean, you were supposed to be here tomorrow. But I can free up some time to show you around tonight." The woman flicked a switch and adjusted a few controls. "It's not that much once you get used to it. But this isn't why you're here, so don't get hung up on it. I'm Cleo."

"You look way too young to be running a place like this," Melissa said, staring through the glass at the activity on the dance floor.

Cleo grabbed Melissa's wrist and let go of it with a smile.

"See? No pulse. You're still getting used to things, huh? You don't have a handle on how to tell whose hearts are still beating and who is…more like you? That's why you're here, isn't it? To find your way out of Blakey's little place and into somewhere you fit in, right?" Cleo licked a long sharp incisor and rocked back in her chair.

Melissa stared back for a moment "Blakey? Sounds like you've known him a while," Melissa said. "Like an ex or something."

"Close enough. You catch on quick," Cleo complimented. "That's good. Things can move pretty quickly around here sometimes. So let's get down to where to fit you in, why don't we?"

"Wait, that's the interview? I don't think I understand," Melissa said.

"Then I'll give it to you straight," Cleo explained. "A couple of my boys went and saw you dance a few weeks ago. They were impressed and got my permission to take you. And the rest, I think you know by now, got…messy."

"What do you mean, your permission?" Melissa asked. "What about what I have to say about it?"

Cleo leaned in toward Melissa. "A lapse in judgment on my part. I was sure I could trust my boys to handle themselves appropriately. If you want to go, you can go."

Melissa chose her words and looked down at the dance floor

again. "I just haven't quite decided what I want yet. I'm not even sure if there's anything I do want anymore."

Cleo stood and placed her hands on her hips. "Well, let me ask a simple question, and you can decide how to handle this. If you stay, you either work with me until we can discover your ambitions, and you can bring your sister along on your own terms. Or, you will be indebted to me for the loss of my boys, and I'll take her for myself anyway, with you as nothing more than a pawn in my game until I can replace you."

"And if I go?" Melissa asked.

"Aha! The door number three option!" Cleo laughed. "Well, if you go, the debt still sits on Blakey's shoulders. I'll handle my business, I owe you nothing, and I don't want to see you back here. I'm not a terribly complicated girl, but I am a bit impatient, so you have til midnight tomorrow to decide. Once my floor show goes on, I'll need to know where you stand. Beside me, under me, or far behind me."

"Why do you want my sister? She barely survived this week thanks to your getting involved in our lives," Melissa accused.

Cleo spun her empty chair and then stood behind it when she faced Melissa again. "Once I make up my mind, I'm hard to budge. And a good pair is not something I'd like to part with. You can't understand how rare it is to collect two talented young beauties at once. But, as for right now, you should make the most of your very limited time. You may see your way out. I'm looking forward to tomorrow."

Digging Up Bones

Tanya sat up with a pillow in her lap, thumbing across her phone screen with only her headboard lamp to light the room.

"So you're sure that's everyone who worked there? No one we missed?" she asked.

"Crazy how you slept like a log last night, and now what is it? Almost three and you're still up and still bugging me. Give it a rest." Blake kicked the pillows at his feet in frustration.

"I told you I would," Tanya said. "All you have to do is let me in a little. We can either talk about her, or I will keep you busy with how to contact the families of the girls who worked for you."

"And I told you," Blake replied, almost snarling. "Every piece of information I needed for that was kept in a filing drawer. Which is gone. Destroyed. There's no way I could know even one emergency contact number, or address, or anything else without that paperwork."

"Fine. So tell me about your mother," Tanya pressed. "Why didn't you ever try to go home?"

"Why are you pushing this so hard?" Blake asked.

"Because I need to know why you'd be willing to risk

everything to find your sister, who you say can't even be saved, but your own mother gets tucked away in the corner of your mind." Tanya stood up and tossed her phone on the bed. She walked around and fluffed Blake's foot pillows again. "Did she hurt you? Was she abusive or unfit or something?"

Blake kept his eyes closed and turned his head away from the light just enough that Tanya could see the pink scar on his neck almost shine below his prickles of red hair.

"You'll be quiet if I tell you why?" Blake asked without looking at her. "Promise that if I answer, you'll shut up and let me get some sleep."

"As long as it's not bullshit," Tanya offered. "I'll give you some peace when you tell me."

He stared up at her through the dim light and breathed heavily through his nostrils. "She walked out on me. She remarried. She had another baby. All in the space of a year or so."

"And Leila told you all that?" Tanya pried.

Blake looked over toward the window that only saw the back parking lot of the building. "No. I found Joan myself when I was still young enough to hope she cared. That was the first time I met Simon. A perfect new son in a perfect new home with a perfect new husband. She was carrying a plump round belly with her perfect baby girl on the way."

Tanya stopped fussing with the pillows and sat on the end of the bed and faced away from him. Quietly, she asked, "How old were you? When she… When Joan left?"

"Fourteen. Just turned. Not my idea of a party," he said.

She closed her eyes as if she could stop tears from coming. She took her time to answer and turned to face him again. "I'm so sorry. That must have been the worst possible day."

"I know you won't understand, but it was probably my best day."

When he saw her mouth drop open with confusion, he put his hand up.

"That's not what you asked me about, though. So turn that damn light off and let me get some shut-eye," Blake demanded.

Tanya slowly rose from the bed and walked to the window to close the blinds. She lingered there for a long moment as if she was still looking through the glass to the outside with nothing but the dim light shining on the vertical shades drawn. She took a deep breath that caught in her chest and was difficult to let go of before she turned to flick off the light.

✦✦✦

Blake left a note for Tanya on the bedside table.

"I'm going back alone. Stay another night if you need to. I'll drop you a line when my phone is back on."

Blake spent much of the early morning buying and updating another much cheaper phone and restarted it with multiple notifications. Three were voicemails from the police department asking him to return their call. Two were from claim agents about his insurance. He scanned through his list of contacts and sent a call out.

"Louie. Yeah, long time." Blake hobbled his way to a bench and watched traffic crawl by on the street. "If you're anywhere near a television, I'm sure you saw the news. Right. I don't know yet, but I need some time."

He put a finger into one ear and nodded as if the man on the other end could see. "I can square things back once the insurance comes through or whatever you need. I just need a few days without police attention. No, no. Nothing like that. I'm willing to go to court and all that. Just have to tie up some loose ends first. It looks bad, but I'm clean. Yeah. Wrong place, wrong time kinda thing.

"I got a tip from a friend. He saw it all. Even has a video," Blake said. "Twenty-first century, right? I can send it to you, yeah. Not sure if you can do anything with it. No, no one I recognize. Right. I appreciate it, Lou. I'll be in touch after it blows over."

He ended the call and sent a message to Tanya confirming his phone was working as he had promised. Then Blake started his slow walk back toward the parking lot where the club once stood.

In the final block of the walk, Blake chose to take the main street to better see the area. He leaned against a nearby brick building to take the pressure off his uneven gait and watched the street until he saw a police cruiser go by and out of sight with the flow of traffic. He felt his jacket pocket for his keys, then crossed the busy street to the tune of impatient, honking horns. He waved back at them as if it were applause for his performance of being an injured pedestrian.

Ribbons of yellow police tape hung on the perimeter of the ruins. Much of what he could see around the burnt and crumbled walls were piles of ash, the twisted and marred remains of the furniture, and the club's interior fixtures. Most of the roof and ceiling had collapsed, and one wall appeared to have been pulled down to make for the safe entry of emergency responders or crime scene investigators.

Blake pulled his keys free and approached the storage container on the edge of the lot while he took another look around. He returned his keys to his pocket when he spotted a woman approaching him. She wore a long overcoat that reminded him of Simon's but it was newer, with less weathering and no patches or damage. Her bobbed, black hair hung in a neat curtain under a red wool cap.

"Some fire here. Did you see it when it happened?" she asked.

Blake steeled his face and shook his head. "I wasn't around, no. The place looks like hell. Did you know one of the girls that worked there?"

"No, I didn't. But I was hoping you might." The woman pulled a gloved hand out of her pocket and reached between her lapels to produce a badge wallet. "I'm Agent Waites. My partner is walking up behind you, Agent Sterling. We're with ATF. This was your business, as well as your place of residence, is that correct?"

"Yeah, that's right. I heard about it on the news, and shortly after got twisted off my bike, so it took me a while to get back down here," Blake said.

"A cast but no cane or crutches?" Agent Sterling asked.

Agent Sterling was a bit shorter than Blake, wearing circle-rimmed glasses under a horseshoe of baldness. He wore a loose Windsor-knotted tie that shared a mustard stain with his pale dress shirt.

Blake eyed the stain. "I thought I was a tough enough guy to do without for now. But if I'm being honest, my hip is killing me from the uneven walk. You guys been up all night waiting for me to get here, huh?"

"Waiting for anyone, Mr. Gentry," Agent Waites answered. "The fire call came early in the evening on Wednesday. Around quarter after six? Can we assume you were in the hospital at that time?"

"Uh, no. Wednesday evening, I was just on my way out of town. I was taking a slow night off to myself."

Agent Sterling broke in. "Looks like you should have stayed

at work, Mr. Gentry. My apologies. Tragic thing like that. We found no survivors on the premises. Just noting that your break in routine cost you some serious injury. Your accident was just down the street, coming toward your workplace, isn't that right?"

Blake shifted his weight and winced more than necessary. "Hey, listen, I got a key in my pocket for this container. There are some chairs inside. Do you mind if I pull one to sit a minute?"

"Do you carry a firearm, Mr. Gentry?" Agent Waites asked.

"I do. It's under my arm here. The permit is in my wallet if you need it," Blake said.

Agent Waites grinned. "We appreciate your honesty, Mr. Gentry. Go ahead."

Blake slowly pulled his ring of keys from his pocket and unlocked the container. The air inside was strong and musty. Blake saw a hand stretched into the light from the open door. The arm attached was dressed in a purple sport coat. Blake reached in and grabbed the arm of a chair whose leather was cracked from age and wear.

Blake set the chair just outside the door before he latched it and hung the open lock. "Glad I didn't have this thing hauled off yet. I might need the furniture and supplies once I figure out what my next move is."

"Your accident, Mr. Gentry?" Agent Sterling pressed.

"I was getting a cup of coffee before the long ride and heard the address pop on a police scanner," Blake answered as he sat carefully into the chair. "I couldn't just leave when I heard it. Still don't know how I lost control of the bike. Must've been the shock of seeing the flames."

"A scanner at a coffee shop?" Agent Waites asked. "Seems a little out of place."

"I like a little diner a few blocks up. It's never busy but always open," Blake said. "It's the only place you can still buy coffee for under a buck, and it's surprisingly not bad. If you guys do a follow-up there, they have a pretty good blueberry pie most of the time too."

Agent Sterling stared down at Blake. "We might just be tempted. Care to take a ride with us and show us the place out of this cold?"

Blake laughed. "Hey, I kinda know the routine. I was in a bunch of trouble when I was a dumb kid. Without an arrest, I won't volunteer to get into the back of anyone's car. Am I being arrested today?"

"Not yet, Mr. Gentry," Agent Waites answered. "But you probably should stay in touch. And somewhere close by. This situation doesn't look very good for you. We'll be looking into this as deep as it goes. But any help you can provide will make things move along much faster so you can get any claims in order for the damages. What would you estimate the value of your business to have been before the fire?"

"Either of you got a smoke? I've been trying to quit, but I got a lot on my plate, you know?" Blake asked.

Agent Waites reached inside her coat and tapped a cigarette loose from the pack. She offered it to him and bent to light it. "What were you pulling in?"

"I have been watching the business for a while," Blake said. "It was doing okay, but we were spending too much on staff. My partner wanted out just recently, and I knew I could buy him out for a very low offer. Our agreement was half now, half later, so I signed him off for sixty grand, and he agreed to eat the cost of repairs from the place falling apart. So I think after the updates, the lease was worth maybe Two hundred thousand. I spruced up the place and trimmed some fat, hoping to see some new clients and more profit. But it's only been a week or so. No time to see the difference yet."

"That seems cheap for the location. Where is your partner now?" Agent Sterling asked.

"It was. I spent everything I had on it. My partner was old school. He didn't like updates. Hell, he didn't like much of anything since the turn of the century."

"How can we reach your partner, Mr. ..."

"Michael," Blake answered. "Michael Laurent. He didn't like cell phones, so I don't have a number for him. He's probably blazing in the sun somewhere."

Agent Waites nodded her head. "We'll look into it. Where can we find you for a follow-up, Mr. Gentry?"

"I haven't decided yet," Blake answered. "Somewhere close and cheap. Is my bike impounded?"

"Seems that way, unfortunately," Agent Sterling said flatly. "I'm sure if you go down to the station and give your statement, they might go easy on you."

Blake adjusted in his seat and stretched out his splinted foot. "I'm in no hurry to get back on. Just want to see if she's worth fixing."

"Have a nice day, Mr. Gentry." Agent Waites said as they turned to go.

Blake waited until the two drove away before pulling his phone again to redial.

"Hey Lou, give me a call when you get this. My problem just got a little bigger."

Concrete Roots

The lake water was still warm beneath the surface. Simon swam his way back to the worn bank where he left his clothes to hang dry on some branches and blew a long steaming breath into the cold morning air. He gathered up the pile and returned to the cabin undressed to hang his things a while longer near the stove.

When he entered the back door, the young girl stood in shock, staring at him.

Simon held his clothes in front of himself and apologized. "I didn't think anyone was awake yet. Sorry about that."

"Oh, they're up," she said, still staring. "Reno and um, Fisher are out checking on some things, and Mama is packing. Does she have a name?"

Simon feigned a laugh at her question. "Yeah, she does. But you'll call her Mama anyway because she's touchy about her name. What's yours?"

Simon carefully slid his arms into his coat sleeves while holding his clothes and then turned around to put his pants on while his backside was covered.

"It's Sam. I'm not a kid, you know? It's not like-"

"Yeah. Compared to me, you are," Simon said. "Tell you what, Sam, the day you're comfortable walking around naked, I might not care about covering up myself."

She looked him squarely in his face and reached down to peel off her shirt. Simon turned away from Sam to knock on a door where he thought Mama would answer.

The door pulled open, and Mama walked out quickly toward the pool table in the center of the room. "Y'all get whatever you got and pack it up tight, baby. We can't stay here any-Child! You better put them clothes back on! We got work to do and Mama ain't got time for no games, now."

Sam rolled her eyes at no one in particular, retrieved her discarded clothing from the floor, and left the room.

"I had almost forgotten what it was like to have a teenager around," Simon said. "Do we know anything about her?"

Mama rolled up some clothing and supplies and packed them deeply into a shoulder bag. "I haven't made time for that just yet. On the list of things I had forgotten about, it's been a while since I've had to say goodbye to a home and look for a new one. And edging on winter too. Been a long time since…"

"I know, Phie."

Simon approached her from behind and placed his hands on her shoulders. Mama exhaled impatiently but straightened her back to give in to his touch and lay her head back against his chest. Her eyes were closed with wet corners, and her hand reached to touch his.

"I don't know what you want me to do. I don't have any stuff here," Sam said from behind them.

Mama quickly took a step out of Simon's reach as he made his way to the kitchen area to stack up which pieces of their camp kit would be necessary for travel.

"That's fine, baby," Mama said. "Just anything you see around you want to take and fits in a bag you can carry. If you need anything else, we'll figure it out on the way."

Simon came back to the table with the kitchen goods and tied the bag closed.

"Teenagers," Simon said.

He looked sidelong at Sam and then back to Mama to see if his comment made her smile, but he couldn't look her in the eye.

"I gotta go back. I caught a glimpse on Tanya's phone when I was driving of where she's going tonight, and I have a bad feeling about it." Simon finished putting his shirt on and slipped into his untied boots.

"I knew you'd say that." Mama zipped the shoulder bag closed and walked around the table to get close to Simon. She raised her hand to his face and stood up on her toes to kiss his cheek. "You come find me as soon as you know Angel's okay. Remind that girl she's welcome in Mama's house any time."

She grabbed the bags and gave one to Sam on their way out the back door.

Tanya took advantage of a long, hot shower after she read Blake's text message and crumpled up the note he left. While drying off, she emptied her purse onto the bed to throw away used tissues and recount her cash before neatly repacking everything the way she liked, with her wallet and sewing kit padding her phone in between. She also removed her apartment and car keys and tossed them into the trash. Then Tanya clipped her keys to a loop of fabric on the inside with the key to her parent's house facing out. It was a custom pink key with a fake gemstone on it that had almost lost its shine from wear.

Instead of calling for another taxi, she dressed in dirty clothes, pinned her hair up tight, and began walking toward a second-hand boutique nearby.

Inside the small shop, she found crowded racks neatly arranged by size and didn't take long to decide on a dress and jean jacket. She also pulled down a pair of leather pants with a button fly that fit snugly on her long legs with a slight crinkle at the ankle. The stonewashed jacket had a patch on the back with a silhouette of a motorcycle, and the sleeves were sewn at a roll halfway up her elbow. The minidress barely reached mid-thigh, in a print that looked like snakeskin.

The material was stretchy above the waist and hugged her hips.

Out of the dressing room, she looked around again for a pair of shoes to match the dress that was comfortable enough to walk in throughout the day.

"I see you found some things you like," the clerk said behind her.

The clerk was much older than Tanya and wore a beige cowl neck sweater draped over her jeans, which were tucked into a pair of crushed suede cowboy boots. Her springy white curls framed her face around a broad, clean smile. A pair of half-moon glasses hung on her neck from a silvery chain.

"Yeah, I love these places," Tanya said. "Every outfit has a story. Can't believe this jacket was here. Is denim out now?"

"Well, I don't know. It may not have been here had I not hung it up just this morning. It was mine." The clerk walked around her and looked her over. "It looks like it fits you better, though." Her voice was velvety with a tiny lilt of age croaking at the start of her words.

Tanya grinned and looked at the boots again, especially at the chain anklet that hung on the outside. "It goes perfectly with those boots. I think you should keep it."

"No, please," the clerk said. "It took me years to even put it on again, and it just doesn't feel like me anymore. And now that I see you in it, I know I chose the right time. If you like the boots that much, I have some similar ones on the wall by the counter. What size are you?"

"Boots would be better than heels tonight," Tanya said. "I haven't had a chance to paint my nails, and it's supposed to be a cold night. Size eight, I think, for boots. Unless they're already broken in well."

"It's true," the clerk agreed. "Fashion and weather seldom mix. It's supposed to snow tonight too. No good for traffic after a big shopping day."

Tanya looked around the store and walked in bare feet to the rack of pants. "It is Friday, isn't it? I'm your only customer?"

"It's still early," the clerk answered. "Besides, we're not a big business with all the stuff people see in commercials. We'll probably see a few in the afternoon. Most likely as soon as I sit down for lunch," she laughed.

"I guess I'm just trying to keep my days straight. Yesterday didn't feel like much of a holiday," Tanya said as she looked out the window to the sunny street.

A twisted tree planted just outside the window rustled in the breeze and cast some shade into the front of the shop. Tanya could see where the roots had grown enough to crack the sidewalk and where branches had been trimmed away to prevent growing long enough to touch the glass.

"That crack in the sidewalk is heading straight for your store. Do you ever worry it might creep in?" Tanya asked.

"Maybe," the clerk answered. "It's kind of hard for me to dislike something just because it has strong roots, though. It gives me some peace to know there's something between me and the street out there. I never really was a city girl. I just never got the gumption to go back home after my husband passed."

"So now you have a strong root grown here, too." Tanya smiled. "Hey, um, is there somewhere I can throw out what I wore in here? They're just not me anymore, either. And they're not clean enough to donate. Would you go ahead and ring these up for me, please? I'll be right there to try on some boots too."

The clerk fetched a bag from behind the counter for Tanya's discarded outfit. She returned to pull the tags off what Tanya was wearing and began punching keys on her register.

Tanya plucked her phone from her purse and sent a text to Melissa as she stepped in front of the window.

"Hey, it's been rocky lately. I'm sorry. I have that interview tonight, and I'm not sure I can do it without you. Please say you'll come with me. I need you. I'll send the address."

Ties That Bind

When Tanya's taxi arrived at the address late in the evening, she could see a line of people wrapped around the corner leading to the main entrance of Shadow Puppets. Wet snow was falling, making the street shine like a mirror in between the slush slowly gathering on its edges. The roving spotlights on the roof of the building had been visible since she reached this side of the bridge across the river. There were lighted poster-sized panels of changing photos of what must have been the inner floor plan. They were inset where they replaced the building's original windows. Some of the patrons were shown in candid captures, and what were likely some of the employees as sort of a living brochure motif.

Tanya tipped the driver and turned to take a better look at the people waiting in line. There were easily over a hundred individuals that she walked past that appeared to be in their upper teen years, and many of them were dressed in what she would describe as typical goth attire. Saturated pale makeup, mostly black clothing, off-mainstream hairstyles, and jewelry with occult symbols. She stood out near the others in her snakeskin print dress and blonde hair she had cropped this afternoon and curled in a similar style to the store clerk she had just met.

There was a loud groan from several nearby teens as she pulled her phone from her purse to show the doorman the ad Blake had sent her. He was burly, clean-cut, and taller than Blake, with a neat chin beard braided and tied with a piece of leather cord.

"I'm supposed to see Lady Cleo about an audition," Tanya said.

He looked down at her phone screen and back at her. He lifted the queue barrier rope for a group of teens waiting to enter and replaced it before pulling his phone out to make a call with his hand up to the crowd.

"Yeah. Got another one who wants to see Cleo. Nah, not like that. A blondie," he said into his phone. "Yes, ma'am." He pressed the screen and slipped his phone back into his pocket. He addressed the line again and looked over a group before lifting the rope.

"Let me see the contents of your purse, miss," the doorman said, looking back at Tanya.

She opened her purse and spread it wide enough for him to see. He gave a nod and nodded toward the entry.

The first steps into the building were like traversing a dark maze with no choice in direction. It was a long, tunneled hallway of draped fabric that vibrated with beats of music and was meticulously, dimly lit with string lights to show the way. Once the space opened up to show the room, she couldn't help but flinch at the change in lighting. Lasers and dancing spotlights shot from around the corners and lofty ceiling making it difficult to navigate at first. Pressure lights on the floor popped different colors in the room as people moved around, enticing their attention to making the tiles change and move like an immense arcade game. The bar area and restroom doorways were the only static bright lights in the main room.

Tanya made her way to the bar, noticing the drink selections were quite slim. Typical soft drinks were offered from a soda gun, bottled water, and a canned beverage called O2 at reasonably cheap prices for an inner city club. She pulled her phone from the clutch purse to check the time and tucked it away, scrunching her lips. The drive to the city seemed to drag on and she still had to wait forty painful minutes before meeting Cleo before the show started.

The beats from the music were throbbing, and Tanya shifted her weight as the vibrations crawled up her thighs. She perused the room of teen cliques and mingling singles but kept close to the bar to avoid the temptation of losing track of time. Only a few people mixed into the crowd appeared to be adults, looking like they were trying the place out or attempting to cling to their youth.

The glowing panels on the walls drew her eyes to a countdown to midnight, allowing her to note the time without looking down or reaching into her purse. After the time reminder flashed away, other pictures of the club's features appeared much like the ones outside. It kept her occupied as she leaned against the bar's edge. The panels showed the club features like the atrium, the dance floor, a live disc jockey, and a runway of models wearing better-fitting versions of the styles many customers wore. The last of the images had her finger curling a strand of hair.

After a few songs strung together, Tanya had just pulled her phone to check for any update from Melissa when she was approached by a young woman dressed plainly in neat, long-sleeved black clothing. "You came to see Cleo?" She wore a large crocheted beret that held her hair out of sight, and her face was pale and thin, with large dark glasses covering her eyes.

"Yes, I'm a bit early," Tanya almost shouted to be sure she was heard.

The woman turned away to walk toward a corner past the crowd near a jutting stage. Tanya followed closely until they reached a curtain where the woman revealed a door to a large room that looked like a storage space. Inside were two other people standing near some blanketed figures.

The room's edges were shelved with fabrics of varying colors, bolts of patterned cloth, and worktables whose backs were pinned with sketches and photos from magazines of varying outfit inspirations. A chain of clothing racks with many empty steel hangers almost cut the room in half near an ironing and steam table. Two sewing machines were fixed into sturdy tables on the far end near a set of supply cupboards opened to reveal threads of nearly any color one could imagine. Rolls of ropes, ribbons, cords, strings, and even metal chains were stored and carefully arranged in a cabinet space on the opposite side. Pens and pencils littered a sort of shallow trough in front of a broad drafting table already fixed in an angled position with a roll of blank parchment pulled across it and clipped into place.

Tanya could barely breathe as the music was dampened to near silence once the door had closed behind them. "This is-"

"Quiet, please," the young woman quickly broke in. She removed her glasses, revealing bright brown doe eyes. She addressed Tanya and the two others as if she were a stiff military training sergeant. "I am looking for someone with a fresh breath of inspiration. Someone who will tend to the needs of a new line of clothing and accessories, possibly to the point of exhaustion. Someone who is not afraid to let their passion for fashion overcome their desire to see the sun. This is the beginning of a career opportunity that will be paid quite handsomely. The hours are long and painful. Your study of the world's aesthetics toward drawing recognition through stitches and seams will consume you."

She pulled at her wrist and removed a small digital watch to place on the ironing board.

"I am Lady Cleo. I am not interested in who you are. Yet," Lady Cleo said. "Impress me with something worthy of wearing for my show tonight. What you'll find behind you, under the covers, are already dressed mannequins. They are wearing a very simple but timeless outfit that I'd like to see what you can do with. This style is perhaps the most resurging in many cultures of civilized modern humanity. I am asking that you help me reinvent the wheel for feminine beauty standards. You have a few hours to contemplate and work in this space. If you find any of my terms unacceptable, you may go now and enjoy the evening. Otherwise, when the timer on this watch sounds, you are finished and will return to the floor to see whose design I have chosen in the only way fashion should be. On full display, with the rapt attention of a full audience. See you at midnight."

Lady Cleo replaced her glasses and left the room with the music beats sudden and jarring after those few minutes without its overwhelming pulse.

The other two left in the room with Tanya looked very excited to get started. They were a man and woman, who also did not trend with the style of the club. The man wore a pair of silver-rimmed glasses with slim rectangle lenses. He was rather short with a wet, brown lay-over haircut that fell slightly over one eye. His lower lip was puffed out with a soul patch, and he wore a dull blue suit whose cuffs at the ankle and wrists were a bit short with the current style. His partner had a high wave of side-shaved pompadour ringlets in a seafoam green. Her scattering of facial piercings drew Tanya's eyes all over as the jewelry caught the light. Her outfit was a belt-backed vest, tight distressed jeans, and bold red high-top sneakers.

"No time to waste," Tanya said. "Good luck!"

She reached for the tarp to pull off her mannequin, and the other two groaned behind her.

"Oh, honey, that's what you have to work with? And with no partner?" The man folded his hands nervously as he spoke and then reached for their tarp. "Oh, you cannot be serious!"

Both mannequins were dressed in a simple, flowing, full-length, white linen gown. Each had a matching black-beaded belt draped around the waist resembling a nun's Rosary.

Tanya checked her phone again for a reply from Melissa and then pulled up some of the pictures she had saved. She flipped through the images quickly and shook her head at each as they went by. When she noticed the other two had gotten started, she shoved the phone back into her purse. Tanya began racing around the room to gather scissors, pins, and measuring tape.

She came back and first removed the beaded belt. She twisted and wrapped it several ways in her hands and formed it into a cat's cradle between her fingers.

The door opened behind them and Tanya jumped at the sudden sound of music blasting again. Melissa let the door close behind her as she slipped a leather jacket off her shoulders and hung it on the corner of the drafting table.

"Hey T," Melissa said. "You look like you're all tied up there. Need a hand?"

Tanya dropped the beads to the floor and ran to hug Melissa.

"I didn't think you were coming," Tanya cried into her sister's shoulder. "Where have you been?"

Melissa pushed Tanya back out of her arms and held her by the shoulders. "Later. We have some work to do, don't we? Instead of string games, wanna play dress-up? Your cat's cradle gave me an idea."

Tanya watched as Melissa looked around to take in what was available. She returned with a spool of silvery rope.

Melissa leaned close and whispered so the others wouldn't hear. "I got a gift from a friend recently. Ever heard of Shibari?"

"No, but can you show me?" Tanya asked. "Here, put on the dress. I hate using mannequins."

"I think this rope will catch the lights out there," Melissa suggested as she pulled the linen on over her clothes. "Here, I'll put a video on my phone so we get it right. We don't have a lot of time."

Tanya watched the way the dress moved on her sister and wrapped the measuring tape around Melissa's waist to pull it in tight. She plucked at the dress here and there to get ideas for how it would hang and how flexible it would be to move in to prevent tearing.

"It's a little small for you." Tanya removed the tape while Melissa punched her phone screen and showed it to her.

"Isn't it always too small on me? Just like you're used to," Melissa said, showing Tanya the screen. "Something like this."

Tanya watched for a moment to get the idea of the bondage-style rope tying used in the video.

"Oh! That's amazing!" Tanya smiled like she hadn't in days and noticed Melissa was staring at her hard as they touched hands together, holding the phone. "What's wrong?"

"Later," Melissa said again. "Unspool this rope and tie me up."

"Wait," Tanya said. "This dress needs a cincher. It moves too much to be fiddling with rope."

Tanya looked through some spools and fabrics and returned with two bolts to compare colors against the white linen. "No, these won't work. They're gonna soak the light."

Melissa looked down and swatted Tanya's backside. "Is that leather? Look at you trying something more my style."

"Yes!" Tanya kicked off her boots and began peeling out of her pants.

"T, what are you doing?"

The other pair in the room stopped to watch as Tanya wriggled on the floor to get her pants off as their mouths hung open. They had already cropped off most of the skirt length at an asymmetrical angle, clipped out the shoulders, and added belts to the figure that dangled like a gladiator skirt. They were holding the belt of beads between them when Tanya stood up.

"Leather will make a nice little shine, just like your rope," Tanya answered.

She grabbed the fabric shears, cut off the legs, and then dove into her purse for her sewing kit. She pulled a seam ripper and went to work carefully removing the center seam from what was left of her pants until the button fly was the only thing to close it in the front. She wrapped the pant-waist around Melissa under her breasts and buttoned the front with some effort.

Tanya asked, "Can you breathe in that? It barely closed."

Melissa ran her fingers over the leather and the buttons. "I'm fine, just like I like it, good and tight."

Melissa began to work the rope into twists and loops as it dangled around her neck.

"Those knots will look better in the back. It'll cover too much up here," Tanya suggested. "Spin it around and I'll bring it back to the front and make sure it's more flattering. While I'm doing that, maybe you could add some lace or something to the cuffs."

The column of knots down Melissa's back pulled tighter once Tanya brought the rope around and began making loops and twists around the waist, up under the arms, knotted between her breasts, and making neat diamonds around the buttons.

"The only way to make it stay tight and keep the knots in place is to go under," Tanya said.

"You mean between my legs?" Melissa asked. "Oh! Do like a butterfly panty and run two lines down. Sort of like a harness. Then you can just clip away any extra or tie it to hang like a bow. Then find a hoop or something to clasp it just above on the front or back so it's easy to get in and out of. I'd gladly wear this the rest of the night, but it's not mine."

"Since when does that stop you from taking what you want?" Tanya asked with a laugh.

Melissa reached for Tanya's hand and held it until Tanya looked up.

"That's not who I ever wanted to be," Melissa said. "Not someone who took from you. Tilly, I-"

"Missy, I know. I was just joking." Tanya squeezed her hand. "But seriously, come home with me tomorrow. To celebrate when we land this new job together. Help me apologize to Mom and Dad for missing Thanksgiving."

Tanya cinched the knot tight between Melissa's legs and made a loop to hold until she could find something to clasp it.

Melissa squished up her face like she did when they were kids when she didn't want to do something. She pushed her lips out to make her voice change like inhaling helium. "The rope is a little bit tight, T."

Tanya ran back to Melissa with a handful of different rings, none of which were quite the size she wanted. She retook the shears, clipped the metal ring off of her purse strap and yanked the rope again to make the fit snug.

"You like it tight," Tanya joked. "Please. If Cleo was honest, we might not get a day off for a while. Come home with me. Tonight."

Melissa relaxed her squished face and looked at Tanya, eye to eye. "I'll come home tonight. But I have a favor to ask in return, okay? Something we can talk about on the drive. Things are different."

Tanya nodded and grinned with watery eyes. "I think I understand." She wiped her eyes on the sleeve of her jacket. "We'll figure it out. I don't want to be away from you anymore."

Tanya pulled the skirting out from the ropes, making it appear to have a fabric curtain on the outside of Melissa's legs.

"Tilly, are you sure you mean that?" Melissa asked just as the watch beeped on the ironing board.

The door opened again, and the music came with it for the first time in the hours that passed. Tanya scrambled to gather the tools she had used to arrange in a neat pile on a sewing table. Lady Cleo walked in and looked over the finished product from both teams.

The other dress had the beaded belt strung around the mannequin's neck and looped under the arms. A series of gold and silver chains hung from the waist over the leather gladiator straps in neatly measured drop lines like icing on a cake. The sleeves were gathered and billowy, cinched in three places to create layered puffs.

"Time's up," Lady Cleo said. "I'll need some time and privacy to get changed for the show. Everyone out. Wait. You're wearing the dress? And you were late."

Tanya began to explain, but Lady Cleo held up a hand and removed her glasses again.

"You'll stay here," Lady Cleo ordered. "I'll get you out of it, and you can properly introduce yourself. The rest of you are dismissed."

Tanya tied up her purse strap, slung it across her chest to keep it more secure in the crowd, and left the room with a last look back at Melissa. Melissa shrugged and offered a smile as she waited inside with Lady Cleo.

Glass Ceiling

Simon had no trouble finding the club called Shadow Puppets, whose front door security was turning away a line of teenagers. He could overhear the doorman, almost shouting, "We have reached capacity for the evening. Remember for future events to purchase reservations to ensure entry."

Around the back of the building, Simon had found a rear entrance that was locked tight with a heavy door, likely for employees and deliveries. Nearby was the bottom of a fire escape leading up three stories. This side of the building had rows of matching windows that likely at one time had been apartments. The lot of them were dark, from vacancy or obstruction from inside, and reflected the streetlights in their dingy panels. He began his ascent after the line of waiting club-goers advanced around the corner, carefully climbing the wet, rusted steel bracings and weak sections of the platforms along the way.

When he reached the rooftop, Simon narrowly avoided being blinded by the swirling spotlights. He made his way to the glass ceiling that looked down into the club's main floor. The changing lights and colors made him wince and narrow his eyes against the assault, but the figures below were all too similar to make out useful details. A harsh gust of wind surprised him, flaring Simon's nostrils. Even with the city smells surrounding him, an unwelcome scent got him back to his feet and running toward the rooftop access stairway door to get out of sight.

Simon moved through the dark hallways quickly. Many of the apartment doors were broken or removed and he could see many windows within were covered from the inside with cheap ratty curtains or particle board. From the look of neglect and disrepair, this part of the building hadn't been in use for at least a few years. Music steadily pounded through the walls.

Simon descended until he found an unlocked door to another long empty passage on the ground floor just as the music stopped. He could hear the crowd chanting something he couldn't quite understand through the walls and made his way closer to the sound. The nearest door he could reach led him to some sort of workshop area for making clothes. It was quite large and organized, packed to eye level around the room with plenty of supplies for the work. A pair of mannequins, one dressed and one empty, were the only things that seemed out of place except for some tools left near a sewing machine that appeared to be recently used.

He crossed the room to a door on the other side to find himself behind a curtain. The door closed behind him, and the crowd chanting a countdown stopped just as he found the seam to look through. The room was dark, other than dim lights on the floor under the feet of so many shadows he could not count. Suddenly, a bright spotlight shone in his eyes as it cut across the room to hit the stage before pointing upward.

Simon shut the curtain and continued behind it to find a better look at the room. From behind the stage, he could see the green glow of an EXIT sign above a door in the corner. He huddled close to the exit door and took a peek out again to see why there was such a hush in the room.

Melissa got to a seat in the control room just as the countdown was ending on the floor below. The switchboard in front of her auto-cued spotlights to shoot across the empty stage and then climbed upward to the rafters just below the glass ceiling.

The lights crossed and focused on Lady Cleo. Her arms were outstretched and her feet close together, much like a crucifixion, wearing the dress Melissa had been in only minutes before. Her body lowered very slowly toward the silent room of shadows veiling the floor lights below. From this distance, Melissa couldn't see how Lady Cleo was doing it. She looked like she was floating in the spotlight as the minutes crept by. Cues on the switchboard were changed to eliminate all but the main spotlight. Melissa could barely see two figures on the stage getting into position directly below Lady Cleo.

Melissa looked over the crowd with her full attention. The shadows did not appear to shift weight or change their posture while awaiting Lady Cleo's descent. When she looked back up at the crucified woman floating downward, she saw the color of the white dress sleeves begin to turn red at the wrist, elbow, and armpits. The contrast looked like blood in carefully chosen positions, making Melissa bite her lip with the sharp fang nearly piercing her flesh.

Tanya joined the countdown, and her excitement could not be contained as she waited to see what the fuss was about. If the music was loud before, the crowd shouting in unison was deafening. There were so many more people on the floor now than when she was escorted to the workshop that her elbows bumped into at least three people while she tried to just stand still.

After downing the unfamiliar O2 drink from the bar, she worked toward the stage. It had been almost half an hour since coming back out, and she still hadn't seen Melissa anywhere. When the countdown ended, all but the floor lights went out momentarily. The crowd made some sounds of protest at first, and then a team of spotlights flooded the stage area, lighting most of the back wall and curtains draped behind it. She saw a hand move the curtain where Lady Cleo had taken her to the workshop and hoped it might be Melissa coming back to the floor just in time for the show.

The spotlights climbed up, and Tanya followed the light and the entire audience's attention upward to a feminine figure wearing the outfit she and Melissa had just finished coordinating. Lady Cleo's hair was a long curtain of black that mostly hid her face as she looked down toward the floor. Tanya was sure Lady Cleo looked directly at her just as the crowd hushed.

Tanya couldn't catch her breath as the silence surrounded her. She couldn't focus on anything but the slow fall of the crucified Lady Cleo. The bright white of the dress began to show growing stains of red as Lady Cleo lowered. The lights were reduced to just one centered spotlight following the descending figure toward the stage.

Tanya blinked hard and looked down for Melissa again but had no luck. All the other crowd faces around her were still looking up. She could see on the edges of the dance floor a few shadows moving carefully closer to the stage. When she looked back to the stage, she saw two burly masculine shadows in place directly below Lady Cleo, standing just behind where small puddles were forming on the stage floor.

Her breath caught and labored as she watched the last moments of falling Lady Cleo but could now see the wires fixed to her wrists, elbows, and underarms, cutting into her flesh to make her bleed and saturate the white linen with large blood stains. She placed a hand on her chest and felt the rise and fall she could not placate.

Lady Cleo's feet touched the floor, and her toes curled into the puddles of blood. The burly figures were illuminated now. They each dressed in dark clothing similar to what Lady Cleo wore earlier that night. Simple, full-sleeved, black clothing fit for backstage work. These men approached Lady Cleo, who was now suspended in place, only barely touching the blood on the stage when the spotlight shut off.

Strobe lighting filled the quiet room and danced all across the space. Lady Cleo in the strobe looked in slow motion as she was lifted carefully from her wire bonds. They eased her to the floor, where she sunk to her knees and slowly lifted her face to the audience to bare sharp fangs and animalistic, shining yellow eyes. She stood slowly on her own, with the skirt dripping wet to match her arms. Lady Cleo spun in the pool of blood and slashed the throat of one of the men. He slumped to the floor with a resounding, heavy thud. The other man stepped forward in the flashing lights and was caught by Lady Cleo with a thrusting palm to his face. She took hold of him as if he were weightless and dipped him over her knee to sink her teeth into his exposed neck.

Tanya could not see the bite behind Lady Cleo's curtain of black hair. As soon as she tried to blink away the lights for a more focused look, Lady Cleo turned her face to the crowd, dripping with fresh blood and bared teeth. The crowd made various uncomfortable sounds and movements as Lady Cleo's laughter filled the room.

The glass shattered from the ceiling, and Tanya recognized the large bodies of several beasts from the night she was chased from her apartment. Snarling and snapping teeth were met immediately by gunfire that crossed the room and pelted the stage. Screams could be heard just before the house music cued again, sending the lights back to a pattern similar to when Tanya first entered.

Tanya was on the floor, crawling toward the workshop room door in the corner while the crowd was pushing in the opposite direction. Some slumped over from getting caught in the crossfire. One stepped on her back as they tried to run and tripped, only to be trampled themselves. The large bodies of the werewolves were out of sight from this low to the floor, but the screams and gunshot sounds kept Tanya crawling.

Glass broke somewhere across the room and she could hear people shouting "FIRE! FIRE!"

Tanya finally found herself separated from the crowd, crawling on her elbows through bits of glass. Next to her, as she crawled, a young girl cried on the floor with a shard of the ceiling glass jutting from her neck. One of her arms had been broken and was twisted unnaturally behind her. Tanya saw the fire spread to the curtain and ran for the workshop door, only to find it locked.

"MISSY! MISSY, WHERE ARE YOU?!" Tanya screamed from the corner and ran behind the stage toward another door. When she found it unlocked, she turned and screamed for her sister one more time.

She could see a line of figures coming toward her behind the dark curtain that lined the opposite way she came. They were cloaked and appeared to be floating closer, faster than she could think. Their eyes were a beastly yellow like Lady Cleo's a few minutes ago. The flames were approaching from behind, and she had no choice but to exit the room and slam the door shut. She saw a heavy extinguisher in the hallway and broke it free to carry with her. Ahead of her in the hallway were two figures going through a door under a sign marked MAINTENANCE STAIRS.

The lights in the hall flickered, and several popped and blew out entirely. Tanya ran the hall length to the marked door and found red emergency lights on in the chilly basement of the building.

"Hello? Is this the way out?" Tanya asked. "MISSY? Is that you?"

She ran through the racks of supply storage and support pillars until she saw the figures again at a set of concrete stairs illuminated by street lights outside. A rush of cold air hit her and sent a chill through her body from her bare legs up.

"MISSY! I'M RIGHT BEHIND YOU!"

Tanya looked behind her and saw the hooded robes of the cloaked figures following her upstairs. With more light, they looked something like nuns, but their faces were hidden by heavy hoods. All but their haunting eyes. She threw down the extinguisher and ran for the open door. At the foot of the steps, the emaciated body of a man was slumped over. The bones of his face showed where there was no longer any skin or tissue there. Just his empty skull under a head of sleek black hair.

She screamed at the sight and, outside the door, Lady Cleo and Melissa turned to look back toward her.

"Oh, thank god, Missy. I'm right here. We made it," Tanya said. "Someone is coming behind me. Just leave the door open and let's-"

A loud thud could be heard as a large beast jumped into view behind Lady Cleo and Melissa, blocking their way out.

Lady Cleo turned and squared herself for a fight. Tanya could only see the beastly shadow mostly blocking the light from across the street. His form shrunk to human-sized, in a long coat and wavy hair that blew across his face with a gust of snow.

Lady Cleo addressed him. "Get out of my way, Simon. You and Blake couldn't stop me when I was nothing. What makes you think you can stop me now, you mangy mutt?"

"Come home with me, Leila. It's over," Simon said as he blocked the way out of the fenced area facing the alley.

"There is no home for me. No home for either of us. Move, or I will have to move through you," Leila threatened. "Blake told me you never stopped looking. How cute of my big brother, who was never there for me, to try to save me now. Who's going to save you, I wonder?"

Simon pulled his gun from under his coat, and Leila pulled Melissa in front of herself. As soon as she did, a shot rang out and Tanya saw Leila's head rock backward as her hair flew up in a spray of blood that splattered across the concrete steps. Leila leaned into Melissa and sank her teeth into her while holding her as a body shield. Simon unloaded two more shots that penetrated both bodies through the chest.

Tanya screamed from the basement. "NO, SIMON! STOP! MISSY!"

Screeching tires came to a stop where she couldn't see and a hail of gunfire rang out. Leila leaped upward, out of sight, and Simon stood facing the stairs as his body lurched with bullets from behind. Melissa's body slumped into the stairwell and rolled over the edge under the rail on top of the man's corpse that rested in the same space.

Tanya ran to Melissa's body as more gunshots rang out. Several ricocheted into the stairwell, and others hit the building exterior. Behind her, an explosion could be heard from somewhere inside the building, and she turned to see the cloaked figures were nearly upon her. She scrambled up the stairs with her hands up, screaming.

"STOP! PLEASE STOP!" she pleaded, throwing herself on top of Simon's body.

She tried to look back through the door and could only see the cloaked, nun-like figures surrounding the position at the bottom of the stairs. A pair of men grabbed Tanya by her arms and dragged her toward their white panel van in the alley.

"Hey, I know these two," said one of the men in the van. "They're friends of mine. Let's grab 'em and get outta here!"

Tanya saw the voice belonged to Mo. He had a rifle in his hands and was loading a new magazine clip.

"I can't just leave them," she cried. "Please help them!"

The building was blazing with fire. Glass broke out the

windows above. Tanya could hear the wailing fire alarm echoing between the buildings. Flames rushed through the supply racks in the basement and nearly filled the opening where she could still see with flickering orange light as she kicked and screamed against the men holding her.

Mo and two others ran from the van and dragged Simon back just before a series of small explosions blasted inside the basement.

"MISSY! MISSY!"

The doors slammed shut on the van and they sped off with a group of men crammed in the back with Tanya pounding on the door windows. She was hysterical and sobbing.

"Hey, hey, hey. Angel, ain't it?" Mo asked, trying to calm her down. "Angel, we can't go back. We gotta get out of here."

She tried to open the back door and got yanked back to the floor next to Simon. Another man reached back to close the door as the van drove on.

Mo tried to be a voice of reason. "We're gonna get you somewhere safe and then check on your friend when we can, okay?"

The man at the door sat down and asked, "How do you know them? They were in the vamp club. We can't trust them. And what are we gonna do with the body?"

"He's not just some fucking body, vato! These are friends of mine," Mo assured the man. "I'm in good with their boss, bro. Just chill. They were just doing what we were doing, but on the inside, like I said we should do!"

The man scoffed. "If we went inside, look where we'd be now. Some plan."

"Hey, Angel. I need you to just breathe a minute, okay?" Mo moved next to her while the others shuffled around to make room. "Listen, we gonna get you home, okay? Where do we need to go?"

Tanya rocked in place, sobbing with a handful of Simon's coat. She shook her head with incoherent words.

Next to her, a phone ringtone sounded off from Simon's pocket. Simon huffed a heavy breath and tried to sit up.

The men in the van grabbed their guns and watched as Simon moved.

Mo put a hand up to the others and looked at the man in his bloodied coat. "Man, you're alive? Guys, do we have some bandages?" He moved to check closer on Simon.

"Get the hell off of me!" Simon coughed.

As Tanya began to calm down, she watched as Simon reached into his pocket and pulled out a flip phone. He snapped his wrist to open the phone and pressed a few buttons.

"Simon?" Tanya blubbered. "Oh my god! How? Simon,

Missy is gone! Oh, she's gone!" Tanya buried her face into Simon's shoulder.

Simon let go of his ribs as they still bled and put his arm around her. He huffed as the phone rang again in his hand.

"Yeah?" Simon answered. "What do you mean? Explain when I get there." He ended the call and flipped the phone closed. "We need to go back."

The man at the door answered, "That place is on fire and about to be swarmed with police. You're out of your mind!"

"Man, you ain't okay," Mo said. "He's right. That place is gone."

Simon let his hair hang in his face and leaned over, holding his bloodied ribs. "Blush," he coughed. "That's where Blake is. That's where she's running to."

Mo sat back down and shook his head. "But there's nothing there. I saw it myself."

Simon shoved his bloody phone back into his pocket after noting the dents and scratches after he fell from the shooting. "After this is done, you guys owe me a phone."

"The hell are you talking about?" the man at the door asked.

"It's either that," Simon said. "Or you can owe me a new gun, and I get to shoot you when I get it."

The men sat in silence for a moment, looking at each other, still in disbelief that the body they dragged into the van was sitting upright and speaking.

"A phone seems fair," the man at the door replied finally.

"Blake has a container on the lot. He's sitting there waiting for her," Simon said as his breathing came easier. "The one you saw climb up the wall and disappear. That's where she'll be."

Mo leaned up to the driver to give directions to meet Blake. "I'll get you the gas money, man. Chill. I owe these guys a favor, and this is it, okay?" He turned back to Simon. "Can I get you anything else? You want us to drop Angel off somewhere?"

"Angel's not leaving my sight til I'm done with this," Simon said.

Tanya sat up in surprise. Her face was still wet and hot, and her breathing stuttered. She looked into his eyes and then held him tight.

"Damn, that still hurts," Simon said. "You guys know anywhere to grab a burger at this hour on the way?"

What's in the Box?

Blake sat in the street with several chairs from his storage container spread out in a circle around a fire in a barrel. Snow had put down around him, making him occasionally shift his seat and shake the snow off his splint. The chairs were set out for a group of homeless people who offered to bring their barrel if he provided them chairs to sit in and something to burn. Supplies from the club gave them not only plenty of items to set fire to, but a small stash of liquor that Blake offered to share around to invite his company to stay longer. He even bought them all takeout food in exchange for one of the vagrants buying him a few cartons of cigarettes that he also offered to share, with a handful of lighters they could pass around.

As it got later into the night, the others had begun to fall asleep in their chairs and were slumped over in different positions to share the warmth of the fire through the cold snow.

After his call from Leila and the one he made to Simon, Blake woke everyone, thanked them for their company, and offered to let them take their furniture and booze with them to bribe them to leave the fire in a hurry.

Blake used the last of his phone battery to shine a light inside the shipping container to move some things around to hide Brandt's body behind what was left of the supplies he had lined up to burn through the night. The snow had become wet and heavy, laying on the sidewalks and some of the lot, but the wind wasn't as harsh anymore. It had become comfortable weather to just sit with his leather jacket zipped up tight over the extra club t-shirts he layered on from a box inside the container.

Blake lit another cigarette and tucked the pack into his pocket. When he looked up, Leila stood in front of him and grabbed him by the throat.

"Comfy big brother?" she asked. "Nice toasty fire to keep you warm while you sit and wait for Simon to bring you my head, huh?"

"I told you I didn't know," Blake croaked against her grasp. "The girl must have told him where she was going. He is close to her. He watches her."

"You have one last chance to impress me," Leila threatened. "Or I'll deal with you next."

She let go of his throat and dragged her fingernails across the scar on his neck that she had given him years ago.

"The trip here took a lot out of me," she said. "I'll need a little nip before I lock up."

Blake sat up straight and shook off his light-headed state from being choked. "There were some urchins here with me earlier. They're still wandering nearby, I'm sure."

"I don't think so," Leila refused. "I've come to like your taste.

Might just be that I trust you better when you're under my influence."

She bent over him and sank her teeth slowly into him. Blake winced hard at the pain of it, unlike before when it would give him an almost euphoric high.

"Dammit! Stop!" he shouted. "It's too much! You're taking too much! My meds thin the blood. Let go… Let go of me!"

Blake slumped over in his chair when she released him. She smacked his face hard several times to see if he'd wake.

"I guess you've given me your last use, big brother," Leila said. "Cling to your last few breaths while the snow falls. Maybe if you're lucky, you'll wake up in the morning and make some new living arrangements for us. Or maybe you'll just pass away in the street from the cold freezing what's left inside you. Sleep well."

Leila walked away from him into the container and began rummaging through the supplies. She laughed out loud after a moment.

"Oh, dear Blakey. You've been a naughty boy, haven't you?"

Blake jumped from the chair, swung the door closed, and cranked the rod lock. He pulled the padlock from his pocket and linked it into place immediately after. Leila screamed from inside and pounded the doors and walls for several minutes.

"YOU LYING BASTARD!" Leila screamed. "OPEN THIS DAMN DOOR!"

Blake leaned hard against the door, out of breath. "Bet you've never been drunk and on painkillers at the same time, bitch. It's not a pleasant experience," he said to no one in a low tone as he grinned. "I hate when someone interrupts me having a smoke."

He hobbled back to his chair to the sound of Leila slamming around inside the container. He popped another cigarette out of his pack to light. He took a long, slow drag and grabbed his bottle from his side. "It ain't my worst day." He spun the lid off of the bottle into the snow beside him and took a drink. "It ain't my best day." He took another, longer drink. "But it's damn close."

***

The van stopped, and Simon climbed out with Tanya. Mo followed, but Simon held up a hand.

"Tell your sister we might be checking in soon, okay, kid?" Simon said.

"You sure you're good? I can sit a while," Mo offered.

"Maybe once your gang drops you off," Simon said. "It might be nice if you'll grab a blanket or two and bring a car Angel can sit in out of the cold. How'd that be?"

Mo nodded. "You got it. I'll be back in an hour or two."

The van pulled away, and Simon carried Tanya in his arms until he reached the chairs around the fire barrel. He bent over her and buttoned up her jacket.

The sound of relentless pounding from the shipping container drew Simon's attention and he looked at Blake. He pointed where indentations were showing near the lock.

Blake took a drink and offered Simon the bottle. Simon shook his head and nodded toward Tanya. Blake offered the bottle to Tanya and she took it from him. She turned the bottle up for a big gulp and coughed hard as soon as she swallowed.

"Slow down. That's all we've got to get through tonight," Blake said.

Blake reached into his pocket and offered his keys. When Simon reached for them, Blake grabbed his hand. "We're done with this tonight. No more hesitations. No more bullshit."

Simon shook his hand and turned to stir the fire with a large charred board leaning against the barrel. He walked over, popped the lock loose, and tossed the keys back to Blake. Blake tried to catch the keys and fell back into his chair, knocking it over, and sprawled into the snow on its broken pieces.

Tanya put the bottle down, followed Simon to the container, and gave a nod.

"Don't open this door until you hear my voice or the sun comes up," Simon whispered. "Either way, it ends tonight."

"Can't you just wait until morning? Stay with me until morning, and then we'll just open the door," Tanya pleaded.

Simon looked over at Blake, scrambling to stand up and then back at her. "No more hesitations. I need to be sure it's over."

Tanya wrapped her arms around Simon, gently pressed her face into his chest, and nodded.

She bent down to remove the lock and watched Simon crank the latch open. As soon as it was, he stepped into the darkness and stood just inside until Tanya had the latch in place behind him.

"You could've just let me go," Leila said. "You could have kept your nose out of my business."

"You are my business," Simon answered quietly.

It was pitch dark inside. He could smell her chalky familiar scent and the fresh odor of a corpse. Simon closed his eyes and let his nose lead him.

"It won't end here, you know?" Leila asked with a stumble in her words. "There are millions out there just like me. And plenty just under your nose."

Simon took a few steps closer, backing Leila into the corner farther.

"And who was I hurting?" Leila asked Simon flatly as she pushed herself back against the wall. "I gave in to their style, music, need to fit in somewhere, and all this broody teen culture that none of them will hold onto once they marry and have children and all that other gushy, boring, existential bullshit they want so badly to be mainstream. And in turn, I just took a little of their money and a bit of their blood." Leila stepped toward him to stop him from moving. "I never took too much, and they were all willing.

"Your brother out there knows from very personal experience that they enjoyed it, barely remembered it, and have no proof of it ever happening. I was solving the problems of every parent in the tri-state by giving their miserable little depressed teens an outlet. And made sure they got a good night's sleep while not spending a fortune on drugs or therapy just because," she added in a whiny child voice, "no one understands them."

"Anything you took was too much. That was the big difference between you and them," Simon said. "They had a chance to grow up and want some of that. To look back on these years and laugh about how it was. But now, you all have the opposite in common. Because of you, now they'll never grow up either."

"You're welcome to cry for them if you want to. But you better make it quick," she threatened.

Leila lunged at him and he stepped back. She nearly fell as she knocked into something in the container. She jumped up and tried again, his hand stopping her at her throat and throwing her to the wall beside them. She rose again, and he missed stopping her. They slammed together into the floor. Simon grabbed a fistful of hair to keep her teeth at a distance and flung her to her back, and then came up to his knees and tossed her to the rear of the container again.

He wiped his hands clean of her hair that clung to the dried blood between his fingers.

"Someday, your kind may be the end of me," Simon said coldly. "Just not today."

Simon cracked his neck and ground his teeth, letting the beast within take him over.

Outside the container, Tanya sat in a chair next to Blake. The banging within the container had stopped briefly and then grew much louder. She reached between them to take a drink from the bottle and passed it to Blake.

"Mind if I try a puff of that cigarette?" she asked.

"I know you're all grown up, but you ain't gonna like it," Blake answered.

Tanya nodded and looked him over. "I don't like whiskey either, but I could get used to it. It's funny the kinds of things you can get used to."

Blake lit a cigarette and passed it to her. She inhaled deeply and made a face while suppressing a cough. Blake couldn't help but grin as he lit another for himself.

The noise inside caught both of their attention with heavier thuds with more time in between. Tanya looked over to see if Blake was watching as the dirty yellow container showed swelling dents that bubbled outward. Before the sounds stopped, the last one hit the door hard enough that the heavy lock bounced and the rod bent outward. Then it became eerily silent except for the crackling fire in the barrel.

Tanya looked hard at the keys in her lap and took another drag, careful not to cough. It took several minutes for her to finish the smoke. The quiet night made it seem much longer. She held onto the butt long after it burned out at the filter band until she heard a knock at the door.

She stood up slowly and dropped the cigarette butt into the fire barrel. Her hands shook as she made a tight fist around the keys. When she got closer, she heard one more knock. She knocked back.

From inside, she barely heard Simon's voice. "It's over."

She almost dropped the keys as she tried to separate the one that fit and bent to unlock it. She took a breath and cranked the latch hard as it was jammed from the fight. She ran back to Blake's broken chair, took a leg to wedge in the latch for leverage, and leaned into it until it broke open.

Blake gave a short chuckle behind her from his chair by the barrel. "There goes my deposit."

Simon emerged from the container with a cardboard box in his hands. He nodded to Tanya and walked by to the barrel, and stuffed the box as deep into the fire as he could with the piece of charred wood. The smell was awful, and Tanya pulled her jacket collar over her face.

Simon bowed his head at the barrel and looked at the sky.

Tanya went closer to him, careful to keep upwind of the smoke. "What about Missy? Is it done for me just because it's done for you?"

"Did he say it's finished?" Blake asked. "In my experience, there's always something else. One mark leads to another. This injury heals just in time to go get a new one. It doesn't ever really end until we give up or they get us before we get them."

Simon came closer to Tanya, away from the barrel, to take the keys. He nodded without a word and looked into her eyes as if looking for something to say. Simon walked back to Blake to drop his keys into his lap. Blake leaned forward suddenly in response and groaned loudly with wide eyes and a gaping mouth. Simon stepped toward him and punched Blake hard enough to knock him over onto his back and into the snow without breaking the chair.

"It's over for now," Simon huffed.

About the Author

Brian Potter has been telling stories ever since the first time he sat around a campfire. He was a published poet in his early teen years. Since then has been telling stories to create games and pursued acting in local theater productions while tucking away notes for stories to write at a later time.

That time has come, and he wants to thank everyone for being a part of his journey.